MW01286845

Cozy Up
to Terror

a novel about a theme park,
mobsters, Hawaiian shirts, and a Yeti

by Colin Conway

Cozy Up to Terror

Copyright © 2023 Colin Conway

All rights reserved. No portion of this book may be reproduced or used in any form without the prior written permission of the copyright owner(s), except for the use of brief quotations in a book review.

ISBN: 978-1-961030-01-5

Cover design by Zach McCain

Original Ink Press, an imprint of High Speed Creative, LLC
1521 N. Argonne Road, #C-205
Spokane Valley, WA 99212

This is a work of fiction. While real locations may be used to add authenticity to the story, all characters appearing in this book are fictitious. Any resemblance to real persons, living or dead, is purely coincidental.

Visit the author's website at www.colinconway.com

For Fats

"How can the same $&@! happen to the same guy twice?"

John McClain (played by Bruce Willis)/
Die Hard 2: Die Harder

Cozy Up
to Terror

a novel about a theme park,
mobsters, Hawaiian shirts, and a Yeti

Chapter 1

Doyle Flanders lifted his arms in the air and roared. "Arrgh!"

The woman's eyes widened. "Oh, my!" She clutched her daughter's shoulders and bent closer to the child's ear. "What do you think, Taylor? Are you scared?"

The girl put her hands on her hips. "Not even close."

"Maybe a little? It's Yango the Yeti—a real-life monster." The mother playfully shook her daughter. "Rawr!"

Taylor cocked her head as she studied Doyle. Then she pronounced with childlike confidence, "Abominable snowmen aren't real."

Doyle lifted his arms higher and roared again. "Arrgh!" It wasn't any more enthusiastic than his first outburst, but he felt a second growl was necessary for this kid. He wriggled his fingers for additional scariness.

"He looks like a wet dog," the girl said.

The mother's eyes popped wider. "*Taylor!*"

"He smells like one, too."

"He does not." The woman looked up at Doyle. "It's not that bad." She whispered into her daughter's ear, but Doyle caught her words. "Take that back."

"No."

Once again, the mother looked up at Doyle. "I am *so* sorry." She angled her head toward the kid. "She's at that age, you know."

The woman appeared to be in her mid-thirties, about Doyle's age. She wore a beige sweater that tightly hugged her shoulders, black jeans that wrapped her hips even tighter, and clunky tan boots that seemed a size too big for her feet. She appeared dressed for a date rather than a day at an amusement park.

Taylor stood on her tiptoes. "There's a man's face behind the teeth. I told you he wasn't real."

Doyle guessed the girl to be about eight. He got good at estimating the age of children while recently working as a mall Santa. The kid wore faded blue jeans and dirty Converse tennis shoes. Her black sweatshirt read *Self-Rescuing Princess.*

The mother stared directly into the mouth of Doyle's Abominable Snowman helmet. "Oh, my." Her broad smile revealed perfect white teeth. "You are a handsome one, aren't you?" She pushed Taylor to the side so she could stand completely in front of Doyle. "How'd you land such a prominent gig? I mean, this is sort of a big deal. Opening day and all." She flipped her long hair away from her shoulders. "I bet you're an actor. Have you done anything on the stage? My parents are prominent supporters of the community theater. We attend a lot of shows."

Doyle shrugged with some difficulty because of the vintage costume's size and weight. "This is my first time."

Taylor threw her arms into the air. "And now he's talking."

"Shush," the mother said. Her eyes narrowed as she leaned even closer to the mouth of the Abominable Snowman. "You're obviously a natural."

"But he broke the fourth wall, Mom."

The woman exaggeratedly rolled her eyes before bending to her daughter. "He broke the what now?"

"The fourth wall. He broke character. That's what they called it on YouTube."

"Again, with the YouTube," the mother said. "Have you ever stopped to think maybe Yango talks?"

"He doesn't."

"How do you know?"

"Because he isn't real, either. They made him up." She pointed to an inflatable Abominable Snowman that stood next to the newest roller coaster at Lone Star Family Fun Time, Lindo Gato's year-round amusement park. "He's a corporate goon."

"He's not a goon," the mother said with exasperation. She turned to Doyle. "You're not a goon." Back to her daughter again, she said, "He's a mascot, honey."

"Whatever. I just know he's not real." The kid sounded more mature than she looked.

"Okay," the mother said, "but what about the real Yeti?"

"They're not real either. I already said. It's like common knowledge. Duh."

For whatever reason, Doyle felt the need to defend his existence. It must have been the stupid costume that brought out these strange feelings. "I'm real," he said.

Once more, Taylor tossed her hands in the air. "Again with this guy." She glanced at the nearby group of kids. They had moved closer to get a better look at Doyle.

"Where do you think they found him?" one boy asked. "The Himalayas or something?"

"More like a museum," a second girl said. "How old is that costume?"

"It's the original Yango," another boy offered. "It's the same one I saw last year."

"I bet he has fleas," a kid suggested from the back.

"Rabies, too," some other girl chimed in.

A bouncing boy near the front said, "The Disney movies make them look way more real."

"Hush," the mother said to the children, "all of you. Be nice." She turned back to Doyle with a broad smile. "We're from Seahorse Prep Academy. Do you know the school I'm talking about? It's super exclusive since it overlooks Padre Island. Anyway, I'm chaperoning today." She took Doyle's paw and shook it. "I'm Sophia. You've already met my daughter. I was a young mother, but you probably guessed that."

If the woman was in her mid-thirties, as Doyle supposed she was, then she likely had the child when she was in her late twenties.

"Anyhoo," Sophia said with a dismissive wave. "It's so wonderful to meet you. And your name is?"

This woman and her school troop were taking up too much of his time. He lifted his arms. "Arrgh!"

"Oh, sure." Sophia nodded toward the kids. "I get it." She winked into the mouth of the Abominable Snowman helmet. "You gotta get back into character," she whispered. "We'll talk later."

The field trip group waited to ride The Terror, an extremely large wooden coaster. It was the park's newest ride and the first new addition in over seven years. The excitement at Family Fun Time was palpable.

Those who experienced the ride today received a free, limited-edition T-shirt that *read I Survived the Terror.* It featured a graphic of a smiling Yeti riding a rampaging roller coaster. Anyone willing to shell out thirty bucks could buy the same shirt in over half a dozen gift shops across the park.

All morning long, The Terror's train of blue cars click-clacked their way up the first absurdly steep hill before zooming down the remaining tracks. The line of eager riders almost stretched to the neighboring coaster, which had almost no one waiting. A sign near the back of the line announced, "You're only 90 minutes away from The Terror!" A park employee updated the waiting time every ten minutes. It had not gotten shorter since Doyle showed up at the line.

Mascots from other attractions were asked to come to The Terror and entertain the waiting families. Besides the Abominable Snowman, there were costumed monsters such as Bigfoot, a werewolf, and a zombie. There was also a frog, a dog, and a raccoon for the smaller children. Each of the mascots had silly names like Sassy Sasquatch, Willard the Wolfman, and Ricky the Raccoon.

Doyle usually would not have donned a costume because he was a park custodian. However, one of the Fun Time actors—a guy they hired just yesterday to wear the Abominable Snowman costume—went home sick immediately after arriving that morning. He must have realized how busy the day was going to be and wanted no part of it.

Mr. Gilbert, the park's manager, noticed Doyle was tall enough to don the snowman suit—it was even larger and heavier than the Sassy Sasquatch costume—and tasked Doyle with wearing it. With the amount of people in the park for the premiere of The Terror, the manager needed someone to play Yango.

Doyle had tried to get out of it. "I'm not an actor," he said.

Mr. Gilbert dismissed his comment with a wave. "It's a costume. You stomp around and growl. Don't overthink it like those other dolts.

They think they're actors, but they're nothing more than overpaid animatronic robots."

The Yeti garb was hot and heavy. According to Mr. Gilbert, the suit was designed when the park was originally built. There were newer and lighter Yeti costumes available, but the owners of Fun Time liked Yango's retro look. That's why they recycled the character for use on The Terror. It also seemed the park's loyal followers loved the nostalgic vibe of the Yeti.

Unfortunately, the age of the costume led to odd aromas. The booties smelled like used gym socks, the body's fur was reminiscent of an old sheepdog, and the helmet's interior reminded Doyle of stale Fritos. At first, he thought it was his breath recirculating back on him, but Doyle couldn't recall the last time he ate corn chips. Besides, he brushed his teeth after breakfast.

Doyle enjoyed the scents around the theme park—the corn dogs, the popcorn, and the funnel cakes. It was one perk of working at Fun Time. He'd only been there for three weeks, so he hadn't grown to detest the aromas like some of his co-workers. But drowning in the Yeti helmet funk all day wasn't apt to put him in a good mood.

Overhead, a speaker crackled before a man announced, *"Welcome to Lone Star Family Fun Time, an independently owned amusement park, located here in beautiful Lindo Gato! Be among the first to experience all the heart-pounding thrills of The Terror, our newest attraction. Wait times may vary throughout the day."*

Doyle started down the line, but Sophia said, "Excuse me, how long is this gonna be?"

He motioned toward the sign with the listed wait time. An employee was updating it again. "Looks like a hundred minutes," Doyle said.

"A hundred minutes," several kids moaned in unison.

Taylor rolled her eyes. "He's still talking. Don't they teach them anything about being the Yeti?"

"*Taylor*," the mother said. "Don't be rude."

"I'm not. I saw that on a video, too. He's supposed to be like Dad—seen, not heard."

A boy moved closer to Taylor. He wore a T-shirt with an image of a cat eating a burrito, black jeans, and green tennis shoes. "I saw that video, too."

Taylor smirked. "Whatever, Ezra."

"No, for real. It was the one where they showed the subliminal snowman."

Taylor's eyes narrowed. "Abominable but go on."

The boy nervously chuckled and crossed his arms. "The people on the show said it was all a misunderstanding about everything and stuff. That's all anyone knows about the abdominal snowman."

"That doesn't make any sense."

Ezra kicked a pebble. "Maybe you didn't see the video I did."

Taylor frowned. "Obviously."

Sophia checked her phone, then looked at her daughter. "At this rate, we're going to stand here all day. Don't you want to try a different ride?"

"No, Mom." Taylor said it in a way to make her mother feel like the stupidest person in the park, maybe the world. "The Terror is the only reason to be here. Otherwise, we might as well have gone to the museum."

"But there are other rides." The mother pointed toward a nearby carousel. "What about The Palomino?"

"The merry-go-round?" Taylor stuck out her tongue. "Do we look like babies?"

"You used to love it."

"No, I didn't." She looked at the other kids. "I never did. I hate the stupid Palomino." Taylor motioned toward a now silent roller coaster. A tall plywood fence surrounded its exterior and hid its base from view. "I used to love The Summit. I rode it all the time."

All the surrounding kids oohed.

"When did you ride The Summit?" Sophia asked.

"Dad took me," Taylor said.

"He better not have."

Taylor shrugged. "He told me not to tell you."

The mother's expression flattened. "I'll have a conversation with him about that." Sophia abruptly turned to Doyle. "I'm divorced." She held up her left hand and showed her bare ring finger to the Abominable Snowman's maw. "In case I forgot to mention that."

Doyle stepped back. "Time to go." He waved at the kids. "Enjoy the ride."

"He's still talking," Taylor said.

Ezra moved even closer to the girl. "So unprofessional."

The mother grabbed Doyle's paw. "Please don't leave."

"I should say hi to the other kids."

"What about these here?" She waved at the field trip kids.

Doyle motioned elsewhere in Fun Time with his free hand. "I meant the faraway kids. Like on the other side of the park."

"Fine." Sophia pouted. "Let me get a picture first." She let go of Doyle's paw and quickly handed her phone to her daughter.

"Mom, no!" Taylor said. "You're embarrassing me."

"Stop it and take my picture." Sophia grabbed both of Doyle's paws and lifted them in the air. "Pretend you're going to attack me. Like really mean it so I can show my friends. They won't believe I met a real-life Abominable Snowman."

Doyle didn't like his picture taken, but since he was in the costume, he didn't see the harm. He didn't sell it like she wanted, though. "Roar."

Sophia's face pickled. "Eh, that's no good." She tapped a fingernail against her teeth while she thought.

"Hurry up, Mom!"

"Wait. It's not like this line is going anywhere." Sophia lifted a finger in the air. "Can you pick me up like you're going to take me back to your cave?"

Doyle scrunched his nose. "I don't think that's a good idea."

"I promise one picture and then my daughter will leave you alone."

"*Me?*" Taylor whined. "Why are you blaming this on me?"

The mother furiously shook a hand at the girl to be quiet.

Doyle had seen all of Fun Time's mascots getting their photos taken with attendees—even that weird-looking raccoon. He never realized how irritating the park visitors could be. It made him appreciate his job of picking up trash. No one ever wanted their picture taken with a custodian.

This was why Mr. Gilbert had insisted he wear the Yango costume today. To meet and greet the customers. What harm could come from taking a picture with this woman?

"All right," Doyle said, "just this once." He scooped her up.

She squealed with delight and wrapped her arms around his neck. Her feet scissor-kicked in the air. "You're so strong."

"Mom," Taylor cried, "stop acting like a crazy person!"

"Take the picture," she said without looking at her daughter. Instead, she beamed at Doyle. "You must work out."

"This is so stupid," Taylor muttered.

Sophia's head jerked toward her daughter. "Do it," she said through clenched teeth. She looked back into the mouth of the Yeti costume. "You're so wonderful for doing this. My ex-husband could never lift me." She continued to scissor-kick her feet. "Not that I'm heavy or anything. If anything, I'm underweight. My doctor told me that before, but you can probably already tell."

"Okay," Taylor said. "Got it."

Doyle started to put her down, but Sophia said, "Take another. Just in case." She rested her head on Doyle's shoulder.

"I already got a good one," the daughter said.

"Just in case!" Sophia grinned at Doyle. "You can never be too careful when a kid takes the pictures. How'd you get so strong? Do you have any brothers?"

Taylor held out the phone. "Done. Here are your stupid photos. I hope you're happy."

Doyle set Sophia down and stepped back. Several women waited for him now. Each had a phone in one hand and a reluctant child in the other. The closest mother announced, "My turn!"

"I need to get going." Doyle pointed toward the other side of the park.

"Oh, that's great. Just great." The woman motioned to Sophia. "She gets her picture taken, but we don't? I think I'm gonna complain to the management about this."

"Hold on," Doyle said. He didn't want to get in trouble with Mr. Gilbert. He liked his new job and wanted to be a team player. "I don't have to leave right away."

A satisfied smile crossed the woman's lips, and she quickly handed her cell phone to her son. "Take mommy's picture." She spun to Doyle and held her arms in the air. "I'm ready."

"For?"

"Lift me up." She jerked her head toward Sophia. "I want the same picture she got."

The line for photographs had grown to roughly ten women now, all with embarrassed children by their sides.

Doyle voiced the only sound he could muster at that moment. "Arrgh."

Chapter 2

Doyle Flanders clomped along The Pathway of Fun as he proceeded through the amusement park. He'd only been in the costume for a couple of hours, and it already felt like he wore a sack of potatoes and a pair of leaden flippers. He lifted his arms in the air and roared, "Arrgh!"

There was no specific reason to do this except to release his frustration. He thought it was something an actor might do, and it seemed a natural reaction for an Abominable Snowman. Besides, no one would think twice about him doing it.

Nearby, a little boy shrieked and dropped his ice cream cone.

"Hey there," Doyle said. He bent toward the child. "Didn't mean to scare you, kid."

Whether it was because of the sight of a Yeti reaching for him or the sound of the monster speaking, the boy jumped backward. His eyes expanded, and he lifted his arms in surrender.

Doyle straightened. "All right now. Take it easy."

The boy did not, however, take it easy. He screamed as if the gates of hell had opened.

"Kaden!" a man hollered from nearby.

Doyle pointed. "Is that your dad?"

"Eat him," the boy said. "Not me!" He ran deeper into the park.

The father approached with a sour look on his face. "Did he tell you to eat me?"

Doyle waved a paw. "I'm sure he didn't mean it."

"It's the costumes," the father said. "He told that darn frog to do the same thing." The man ruefully shook his head. "That's the second ice cream cone he's dropped. Now, I've gotta go catch him. I didn't know I would be exercising this much today." He trotted after his son.

A steam organ played a jaunty tune as another roller coaster click-clacked its way to the top of a hill. Families jostled by Doyle to get into various lines. Some visitors smiled or waved at him, but most ignored the costume. To many customers, Yango the Yeti was part of the experience and nothing to get excited about.

A balloon popped a moment before something whizzed by Doyle's head. There was laughter off to his right and he turned to look.

A group of teenage boys stood near a funnel cake stand. All were tall and strong looking. Based upon the letterman jackets they wore, Doyle assumed they played on a high school football team. The dopey looks on their faces didn't hurt that assumption, either.

One of them reared back and threw a piece of funnel cake. It might have hit him, but Doyle couldn't feel it because of the costume. The group of boys laughed. One of them jumped and waved his arms above his head like he was a chimpanzee. He mimicked ape sounds as he moved about.

Another teen raised his arm to throw something.

An electric motor whined just before tires screeched. Doyle turned to see a security guard, Ainsley Sutherland, jump from a golf cart. "Stop!" she hollered. "Or I'm gonna run you out of the park for causing a nuisance!"

She hurried between Doyle and the teenagers. Ainsley was about a foot shorter than him normally, and she was much shorter while he was in the Yeti costume. She wore a tan and brown uniform. Paraphernalia of the security job hung from her leather duty belt—a radio, handcuffs, and an overly large water bottle. She pointed at the teenagers like a scolding mother. "What are you waiting for? Move it or lose it, busters."

The teenagers muttered their displeasure at Ainsley for interrupting their fun, but they didn't challenge her authority. The one who was about to throw the funnel cake shoved the fried dough into his mouth.

She turned and looked into the jaws of the Yeti helmet. "Good thing I arrived, huh?"

"Good thing," Doyle agreed.

"Hey, it's you!" Ainsley smiled. "Where's the new guy?"

"He went home sick."

She straightened and glanced around. "He did? I thought I just saw him. I must be hallucinating." Her attention returned to Doyle. "Porter's sick, huh?"

"Mr. Gilbert said he showed up for work but had this strange look about him."

"I guess that's what happens when you aren't feeling well."

"So he sent the guy home so as not to get anyone else sick."

"That's real nice of him to worry about the kids."

"Yeah," Doyle said unenthusiastically, "since they're the ones not buying the tickets."

Ainsley continued to scan the crowd. "That's weird. I could have sworn I saw Porter, like, fifteen minutes ago and he looked okay to me." Her gaze eventually settled back on Doyle. "Why'd they put you in that getup? You're not an actor."

Doyle motioned toward the newest roller coaster. "Gilbert figured it was more important to have costumes than custodians today, and I'm the only one who could fit this rig."

Ainsley laughed. "Well, it's not like I could wear it." She nodded. "That makes sense now. I ran into Oskar a bit ago. He was all twisted up over Gilbert raiding his staff. He must have been talking about you." She stood on her tiptoes to get a better look into the Yeti's mouth. "You like wearing it?"

"Not so much."

"Does it stink in there?"

"Like a bowl of Frito pie."

Her nose crinkled. "It's funny they recycled Yango for the new ride after they had him associated with The Summit for all those years.

I'm sure they did it to save money on a mascot designer or something, but don't you think that's like saving a handful of pennies after spending millions?"

Doyle waved a paw. "That's above my pay grade. I only do what I'm told."

"That's the attitude." She patted his shoulder. "This is your big break, Doyle. Impress the boss and you'll never have to go back to picking up trash."

"I don't mind it."

"It's litter, Doyle. No one wants to pick it up. I'll see you around." Ainsley thumbed over her shoulder. "Don't let punks like that bother you. Tell them to knock it off or come get me and my guys. You don't have to put up with that kind of garbage." She grinned. "See what I did there?"

Doyle forced a smile. "You're a regular comedian."

"Nah. I'm just a theme park hero. We need to have our witty banter down. Hate to run. We're understaffed on the security team today—just me and the goofballs. Couldn't happen at a worse time. I got my fingers crossed nothing crazy goes down. Catch you later."

As Ainsley headed off into a mass of people, Doyle thought about her earlier words. He didn't mind emptying trash cans or picking up the litter. It was mostly mindless work, but the weather was nice in southeastern Texas, and he spent most of his days outside. Also, he didn't have to interact with the public. No one ever walked up to a custodian to start a conversation. They might mention a trashcan was full, or a toilet was plugged, but no one seemed intent on starting a lengthy discussion. He'd had many jobs in his life and this one wasn't so bad.

Right now, it seemed much better than being a mascot.

Overhead, the speaker crackled before a male voice came on. *"Hello Family Fun Time visitors! Stop by one of our conveniently located shops to purchase your officially licensed Yango the Yeti merchandise. We have T-shirts, water bottles, baby pacifiers, and more. Grab something to commemorate your ride on The Terror!"*

Throughout the park, people screamed with excitement as numerous roller coasters and rides whipped them about.

Doyle considered returning to The Terror, but the waiting line hadn't diminished at all. In fact, it had grown longer. He should probably get over there and entertain the crowd. That's why Mr. Gilbert insisted he wear the costume. However, Sassy Sasquatch and Freddy the Frog were already over there. What would adding another mascot do? Nothing, he figured.

Besides, he worried there might still be some overeager mothers who wanted pictures. He could do without that kind of attention.

If Doyle played his cards right, perhaps he could spend his day traipsing around the park and never really do anything. He'd gotten used to the aroma of stale Frito chips inside the Yeti helmet. Perhaps he could just walk and wave and do his best to stay out of trouble with Mr. Gilbert.

He occasionally said, "Arrgh," at a moderate level. He didn't want another repeat of the frightened boy dropping his ice cream cone. Doyle passed rides such as Ricky Raccoon's Bumper Car Challenge, Sassy Sasquatch's Tower Drop of Doom, and Freddy the Frog's Boat Ride of Love.

When Doyle followed The Pathway of Fun back to The Summit, he paused to consider the attraction. An oversized version of Yango hung from the side of the roller coaster. An eight-foot-tall plywood wall ran the perimeter of the attraction. Various signs were plastered to its sides. *Dangerous—Do Not Enter. Restricted Area—Hard Hats Required. Union Labor is Happy Labor.*

The gate's safety hasp remained closed, but an opened lock hung from the ring. A work crew had been inside for the past week. Since Fun Time never shut down for an off-season, the crew had to dismantle The Summit while the park remained in operation. Doyle hadn't been inside the restricted area yet. There was no reason for a custodian to go in.

"Fancy meeting you here," a man with a deep voice said. Something hard jammed him in the right side.

Doyle tried to look, but something hard now poked him in the left side, too.

"Well, well, well," another man said. His voice was smooth, as if he might have been a disc jockey. "We been looking for you, Bumble."

The Yeti helmet blocked his view of both men, but he had a pretty good idea of what was jamming him in the sides.

"Open the gate and step inside," the man with the smooth voice said. "And don't do nothing stupid."

Doyle tried to pull the lock free from the ring, but the costume's paws made it impossible. A hand came into view and slipped the lock away. Doyle didn't try to do anything heroic.

First, one of the guns poking his ribs might have gone off. Second, the costume would have made fighting difficult. Third, if he broke free, he couldn't run anywhere fast.

He thought about yelling, but what would that have sounded like from inside the helmet? Would anyone besides himself hear his cry for help? It was unlikely with all the other noise in the theme park. He had to hope a park visitor might notice two men forcing Yango the Yeti into a restricted area.

Although, this was Yango's former ride. If anyone saw the mascot going inside, they might think it was a final promotional event. Perhaps a photo shoot.

Maybe Doyle *should* fight back.

One gunman opened the gate, and the other shoved Doyle. He stumbled forward. His arms windmilled as he worked to catch his balance.

Unfortunately, the heavy booties he wore dragged behind him and Doyle fell on his face.

The Frito-smelling helmet smacked against his nose and Doyle made the only sound he could think of at that moment. "Arrgh!"

Chapter 3

"Arrgh!" Beau Smith stood abruptly, and his metal chair skittered away. He threw his hands into the air. "What you're saying doesn't make any sense!"

"It makes perfect sense," U.S. Marshal Lester Krumland said. "Please sit down." He calmly interlaced his fingers and rested his forearms on the edge of the table. Krumland blinked several times behind round, wire-rimmed glasses. He was going bald and tried to hide it with a bad comb-over. The overhead lights reflected off the exposed portions of skin underneath the strands of black hair. "I don't get what's so hard to understand, Beauregard. Marshal Goodspeed is out."

"She was here this morning."

"And now she's not. Let's continue."

"Just like that?" Beau snapped his fingers.

Krumland nodded curtly. "As you say."

Lester Krumland was a large man. When Beau first walked into the room, Krumland offered his hand. That's when Beau realized the two men stood eye to eye. The marshal wore a dark suit with a light blue shirt. A gold clip held his tie in place. The suit wasn't tailored—it was purchased on a marshal's salary, after all, but the man wore it with pride. A small American flag was pinned to his lapel.

"I can't believe it," Beau said.

"That I'm your new witness inspector or that she's gone?"

Beau had spent the previous two days with Marshal Gayle Goodspeed. They had traveled from outside Eagle's Feet, Wyoming to this Texas military base. She said they were going to Fort Hood because of worries they had been followed. It was an odd statement because, when they first left the Cowboy State, she had no concerns.

However, Goodspeed clung to that assertion and claimed the large military compound would give them the best chance of losing whoever was tailing them. Beau frequently checked his side mirror but saw no one.

Goodspeed also indicated they would pick up his new identity at the base and get him ready for his next home and job, per the program specifications. Thinking about it now, she was more peevish on that trip than her usual self. He assumed it was because he blew yet another identity.

Secretly, Beau hoped Goodspeed would set up his next placement to be on the Army base. He would have loved to spend time around tanks, helicopters, and the other cool toys soldiers got to work with. Maybe he would have a chance to blow some stuff up.

Instead, Beau now stood in a Judge Advocate General's interview room and studied his newest witness inspector. Obviously, the location was chosen for other reasons and by someone not named Goodspeed.

Krumland opened the thick folder sitting in front of him. "The sooner you accept she's gone, the better it will be for both of us."

Beau turned and looked into a large mirror built into the wall. He imagined someone standing on the other side. Was Goodspeed watching this interview? Or was it Krumland's boss?

For a moment, Beau considered his reflection. He looked nothing like the long-haired biker he used to be. His hair was short, and his long, scraggly beard was gone. He had a couple of days of stubble due to all the driving. He rubbed his chin as he studied his face.

"You didn't force her to retire, did you?" Beau asked.

"I didn't force her to do anything."

Beau shook his head. "The service, then—did they force her to retire?"

"They transferred her. She's still working. Although, at her age, she should really consider calling it a day."

"What about Onderdonk?"

The marshal looked up and caught Beau's reflection. Irritation flashed in the lawman's eyes. "What about Theodore?"

"If Ted's healthy," Beau asked, "why can't I work with him?"

"His track record was no better than Goodspeed's."

Beau turned around to look directly at the marshal. "My blown covers aren't any more his fault than they were hers."

"And yet, it all happened during their watches." Krumland motioned to the opened folder. "Let's begin."

"Your bosses are blaming them for what happened to me?"

"Please, sit. We have a lot to get through."

"Wait. Do your bosses think I could have avoided blowing my covers? They don't think it's my fault, do they?"

Lester Krumland crossed his arms. "How could it not be? You're an anomaly, Beauregard."

"An anomaly?"

"In other words, you've become a rock in our collective shoe."

Beau didn't like how that sounded.

The marshal cleared his throat. "Most witnesses in our program only have a single cover. They spend the rest of their lives in anonymity, with no problems. I'll make the allowance for the occasional complication, which results in the need for a relocation and a second identity. That happens, and we understand it, but it's a rare occurrence. You have had six identities in a matter of months. In fact—" The marshal flipped to the beginning of the file. "Yes, right here. You ruined your first identity in less than a week. How does that even happen?"

"There was a mob enforcer."

"You didn't need to get involved."

Beau's face reddened, but he remained silent.

"It was a marshal-owned business, too." Frustration laced Krumland's voice. "Do you know the cost involved setting something like that up, maintaining it for all those years? Then you waltzed in—"

Beau's lip curled. "I've never waltzed anywhere."

Krumland recrossed his arms. "You waltzed in and botched that business. In less than seven days, I remind you."

"My life was in danger."

"Because you got involved, which, I repeat, you did not need to do. You could have stayed in the background and let the local police handle things."

Beau laughed a sharp, single bark.

"The impact of your decisions has a multiplier effect. Have you ever stopped to consider that? Now that they've outed the bookstore as a marshal-related business, we have one less place to locate a witness. We either must buy a replacement business, cultivate a new relationship, or develop deep cover paperwork. None of those are easy, mind you, and it's more work for someone in headquarters."

"I survived, if you haven't noticed."

"I read the report. You would have been killed if Marshal Onderdonk had not shown up."

Beau looked away. The walls of the interview room were boringly white. Outside, photographs of men and women in uniform and other military paraphernalia hung on the walls. The room's stark nature was a reminder of the trouble some people found themselves in.

"You put yourself in danger," Krumland said, "and Theodore wound up with a permanent mark in his file for getting you out."

How could Onderdonk get a negative review in his file for saving someone's life? Beau turned his attention to his own file. How many marks were in there? Would they kick him out of the program if he got too many?

Krumland flipped through several pages in the folder. His finger stabbed something. "Then you went off the grid for a week? What was that about?"

"I was trying to avoid the Dawgs."

"You're lucky I wasn't your inspector then."

"I'm sure."

Krumland's head jerked up. "What's that supposed to mean?"

"Nothing."

"You pull a stunt like that—go missing for a week—and I'll revoke your agreement and put you back in prison." Krumland nodded emphatically and some wisps of hair fell down his forehead. "I'll do it. Don't think I won't. I'm not letting you derail my career like you did Theodore and Gayle."

"I derailed their careers?"

"Like you care."

Actually, he did. Beau hadn't expected to like either marshal, but he developed a strange affinity toward both of them. Each had helped him escape the Satan's Dawgs multiple times. And Onderdonk had taken a bullet in California when his former crew showed up looking for Beau. It was downright heroic, he had to admit.

He had turned against the club when an FBI agent found the one weakness he had—the love for his grandmother. Beau used illegally obtained funds to pay off her house and renovate it. The agent threatened to prosecute Beau's grandmother and seize her home. To avoid that fate, Beau flipped and ratted on the club.

It wasn't hard to convince him. Beau was the club's bookkeeper—a coded reference to enforcer. The Satan's Dawgs used lots of codes just in case the wrong ears were listening. Beau's job was to keep book on those who wronged the club. He would occasionally have to clear the books. He would do that by many methods—some of them temporary, some of them permanent.

He didn't like the man he had become, nor did he like how the club morphed into an entity that rewarded profit over loyalty. So, when the FBI came calling with its offer to provide information, he took it. Maybe a little too willingly. Remembering his actions soured Beau's disposition.

"Well?" he asked. "What happened to them?"

Krumland harrumphed and pushed the strands of hair back into place. "They assigned Gayle to desk duty in Boca Raton. They put Theodore in Minneapolis."

Beau cringed. "Minnesota?" It was the worst fate Beau could imagine besides prison.

"I don't think I like the way you say that." Krumland shifted in his chair. "It's God's country."

He wondered why people always claimed the worst parts of the world were God's country. Surely, God's country included fun places like Las Vegas and Tijuana. Although, now Beau was trying to be a better man, he probably should stop thinking like that. He would never embrace the idea God actually claimed Minnesota as something he was proud of.

Beau grabbed the chair and returned to the table. "About Goodspeed and Onderdonk. What did they do that was so bad?"

"They failed to control your actions."

"How could they get in trouble for what I did? I was trying to stay alive, trying to stay out of jail."

Krumland flipped through Beau's file. "Must I remind you how many times you've been on social media? You're in witness protection, Beauregard. You're not an influencer."

"There's a perfectly good explanation for every one of those times."

The marshal clucked. "You're supposed to be hiding, but you've got a social media presence rivaling a Kardashian."

He didn't know what a Kardashian was, but he said, "It can't be that bad."

"Are you kidding?" Krumland's finger tapped something in the file. "It says here a video of you fighting some skateboarders in Costa Buena went viral."

Beau bobbled his head. "There was that."

Krumland's finger slid down the paper. "And then there was a video of you in a standoff with the Purple Hat Coalition. That was also in Costa Buena, I might add."

"I think you're misreading how that went down."

The marshal lifted the folder and showed Beau a screenshot. "They're old ladies, for crying out loud. Why would you pick a fight with them?"

"They started it."

Krumland waved him off. "Then there were videos of you fighting as Santa." The marshal showed him another screenshot. "Santa!"

"That's fair. It probably wasn't my best decision."

"Then there was your appearance on the motorcycle review channel."

"Okay." Beau threw his hands in the air. "That one wasn't my fault. If you watched it, you could see I didn't want to be there."

"But you were, Beauregard, you were. The Satan's Dawgs are a criminal biker gang. If they're going to watch any type of videos, which do you think they'll be?"

"Maybe they didn't see them."

"Keep telling yourself that." Krumland fell back into his chair. "And I probably shouldn't even bring up the two marshal hotlines we flushed down the toilet because of you."

"I'd appreciate it if you didn't."

"Two." Krumland held up as many fingers. "Think about all the hours it took to set up those emergency numbers and alert all the assets in the field."

Beau smirked. "I thought you weren't going to bring it up."

"It was too big of an issue not to."

"Uh-huh."

"The problem is obvious."

Beau remained silent.

"Do you see it?"

"You're going to say it's me."

"Of course, it's you. You're in the middle of it all."

Beau didn't like this new guy. "Can I get a different inspector?"

"No, and trust me, it's not like I didn't try."

"If I'm so toxic to a career, why were you assigned to me?"

Krumland cocked his head. "Why do you think?"

"I don't know." Beau waved his hand about. "Because you're supposed to help correct my behavior or something?"

"Let's go with that." Krumland closed the folder. Underneath it was a smaller file. "About your new placement."

"Hold on." Beau felt a rush of excitement.

"No."

He leaned over the table and searched Krumland's eyes. "You weren't assigned my case to bring me in line."

The marshal ignored Beau. He pulled a paper from the file and snapped it. "Ever been to Lindo Gato on the Gulf of Mexico?"

The mention of going somewhere warm almost derailed Beau, but he stayed with his train of thought. "They assigned you to be my witness inspector because you're on the hot seat, too. Someone is setting you up to fail."

"It's not a marshal-owned business, so you're gonna have to be extra careful not to expose your identity."

Beau dismissed the lawman's warning. He knew he was on the right trail because Krumland avoided looking at him. "What'd you do?"

The marshal ignored his question. "No shenanigans like you pulled at your other placements. Got it?"

Adrenaline buzzed through Beau's veins. If this marshal was on the hot seat, too, maybe he would get some preferential treatment. Neither Onderdonk nor Goodspeed ever gave him special consideration. "C'mon, Krumland. What did you do? Why do they want you out?"

The marshal kept his head down. "The weather will be nice, and you'll get to work outside."

"Who'd you tick off?" Beau leaned in and tapped the table. "You can tell me."

U.S. Marshal Lester Krumland pointed to a note. "Gayle approved this placement, by the way. She said it was her going away present to you. This is her endorsement here."

Beau cocked his head and tried to read his former witness inspector's handwriting, but the file was upside-down to him. "What'd she write?"

Krumland bent over the report. "Beau should thrive in this environment—"

"That's nice to hear."

"—since he's so good with children."

Beau straightened and blinked several times. "She didn't."

Chapter 4

"Get up," the smooth voice said.

That was easier said than done while wearing the Abominable Snowman costume. Doyle Flanders pushed himself off the ground and brought his knees up to his chest. The heavy boots dragged, and he felt a pull in his abdominal muscles.

Doyle was still in decent shape, although he hadn't worked out in some time. He used to lift weights while in prison—it was a good way to kill time. The Dawgs had some rusty equipment they kept behind the clubhouse that he would push around now and then.

When Doyle righted himself, he took in his surroundings. He was on the other side of the plywood fence, which put him underneath The Summit. It was his first time being there and it sort of fascinated him, even if it was the wrong moment. He'd never seen a roller coaster being dismantled.

Steel girders and smaller beams were stacked in separate locations. Tools and helmets were tossed in a haphazard pile. A massive Yango the Yeti still clung to what remained of the ride. The workers had torn off the back portions of its plastic legs and exposed the wire framing underneath.

Some calliope music played through overhead speakers. Nearby park rides continued to elicit the cheers and squeals of delighted children. He imagined the aromas of popcorn, hot dogs, and fried food drifted into this cordoned off area, but the stale Frito stench in the Yeti helmet blocked them out. Even though The Summit was in its final days, family friendly fun continued on the other side of the plywood barrier.

A dismantled train of faded red two-seaters sat in several rows. The legacy of this ride was pathetically drying in the wintry Texas sun.

"Now, grab a seat." The gunman was white, in his late thirties, and big. From this distance, Doyle imagined the other man to be roughly the same size as him. The gunman's Hawaiian shirt billowed under the armpits, and his khaki shorts fell too far below his knees. Black sock garters wrapped around pale legs and his oxfords were polished to a high shine.

Outside, two men had braced Doyle. He wondered where the second man was now.

The gunman motioned his pistol toward one of the roller coaster cars. "Move it, Bumble."

Doyle pondered how the Satan's Dawgs managed to find him here so quickly. He hadn't done anything to blow his cover. Since arriving in Lindo Gato, he had followed the three simple rules that Marshal Onderdonk had given him when he first entered the program.

Do not contact people from your old life.

Do not visit places from your old life.
Do not develop habits from your old life.

Even though Doyle wanted to reach out to a woman he thought about daily since his first placement—Daphne Winterbourne—he didn't. That could be dangerous for her, and he certainly didn't want to bring more harm her way. He did enough of that while in Maine.

So how did the Dawgs find him after only three weeks in Lindo Gato? What mistake had he made? Doyle's mind raced, but he couldn't think of anything.

He reluctantly moved toward the first two-seater. A logo for The Summit was splashed across its front—it featured a roller coaster with Yango the Yeti swiping at its first car. Doyle climbed in and sat. It likely would have been uncomfortable because of his regular size, but the suit made it unbearable.

The gunman moved closer. "Imagine our surprise when we heard you were here."

Doyle lifted his hands. "You got me."

"That's right. We do. And when the boss gets his mitts on you, he's not gonna be as gentle as we were."

Boss? Doyle thought. Nobody in the Satan's Dawgs was referred to by that term. Maybe this wasn't about his old club after all. While in Maine, he got crossways with a local mobster. It led to Doyle's blown cover and the gangster's crew looking for him. Perhaps this was related to that.

The gunman's phone rang. He looked down as he retrieved it from his pocket. Not that it would matter, though. Doyle couldn't jump free of this coaster seat and cross the distance to the guy before he lifted his head and fired.

"Yo, it's Tony," he said after he answered. "Uh, right, I hear ya."

Doyle slid toward the edge of the roller coaster car.

"What?" The gunman eyed Doyle. "It's not like he's gonna tell anybody." He rolled his eyes. "Who's he gonna tell? He's right here, all by his lonesome."

Doyle put one heavy foot on the ground.

Tony pointed the gun at Doyle and angrily shook his head. "Okay, I hear you. I won't say my name next time. I didn't say yours, did I? There you go. Listen, did you call for some other reason besides giving me an earful about my phone etiquette?"

Doyle put his paws on the car's handrail. There was no way to quickly leap out of the seat and run over to Tony. That could never happen. His goal was to simply stand. If he could do that, he would be one step closer to freedom.

"Right," Tony said. "We'll be here. No problem. I promise not to do nothing stupid until the boss arrives. What? What'd I say *now*?"

Doyle stood.

Tony excitedly waved the gun as an indicator for Doyle to get back into the roller coaster car. Doyle ignored the motion though and lifted his arms into the air. He didn't roar, though.

Instead, he yawned and stretched with an exaggerated arch of his back. He wasn't sure how much of the effect was lost on Tony due to the costume, but he was pretty sure he couldn't see or hear the yawn because of the Yeti helmet.

"Okay, okay," Tony said. "I won't do *anything* stupid until the boss arrives. Is that better, Mr. Grammar Police? What? What now?"

Doyle took one giant step toward Tony but stopped. He animatedly stretched his hamstring. Or was it his quadricep? Doyle wasn't really focused on which muscle group was being pulled, as he was concentrating on how to slowly get closer to Tony.

The gunman angrily motioned the gun toward the disabled roller coaster. His cheeks were bright red now. "Yeah, yeah. I hear the difference. I won't do anything. I agree—that is better without the stupid. You're right. Makes me sound more intelligent. Listen, I gotta go." Tony hurriedly ended the call. He looked down as he tucked the phone back into his pocket and the gun drooped.

Doyle stepped forward once more.

Tony lifted his head and hurriedly pointed the gun. "Stop right there, smart guy. Take another step and I'll blast you."

"I'm only stretching. This costume is murder on a guy."

"I'll murder you if you keep moving forward."

"But the boss is coming."

"I'll tell him you made a play for my gun. He'll understand."

Doyle straightened. He was still too far away from Tony to make any real kind of move. The park noises drifting over the plywood wall might drown out his calls for help, but they certainly would not cover a gun firing.

"If you pull the trigger," Doyle said, "everyone in the park will hear."

"They've been dismantling this thing all week." Tony swung his weapon toward The Summit. "They'll think it was just a bolt gun. *Pop, pop.*"

"They're taking bolts out. Not putting them in."

Tony shrugged. "That's a good point." He reached into his pocket and removed a silencer. He screwed it on to the end of the pistol. "Any more complaints?"

Doyle should have kept his mouth shut. A thought occurred to him then, and he looked around. "Where *is* the crew?"

"Labor holiday."

"It's Thursday."

Tony smirked. "Unofficial. The boss wanted a private place for us to talk on site, so he called in a favor. We appreciate you making it easy to get you inside here."

Doyle was out of options. The boss was on his way, which meant there was likely more muscle nearby. Maybe the boss even called the Satan's Dawgs, and his old club was riding in from Arizona.

Shortly after he entered the Witness Protection Program, Doyle learned his former crew contracted with someone in the mob to get him on their informant tracking website—thefbiisabunchofdirtyrats.com. Doyle found various pictures of himself under a banner of Rat. Some of the photos were digitally altered to show him with short hair, blond hair, and even bald. It was a disconcerting moment because he never wanted to imagine himself without hair.

So it wasn't a stretch of his imagination to think the mob knew he was in Lindo Gato and they'd already contacted the Dawgs. Doyle wondered how long the ride from Phoenix would take and if this group would keep him alive until they arrived.

He scanned the ground for something to throw. There was nothing nearby. The metal girders and steel beams were too big. He could take off one of the costume's paws, but that would be a mere distraction. The booties were heavy enough and would certainly do the trick, but he couldn't get one of them off in time.

"Why don't you take off that helmet," Tony said, "and let me see that beautiful mug of yours?"

And there it was—Tony handed Doyle his opportunity for salvation.

Doyle said, "It'd be my pleasure."

Once he got the helmet off, he'd have something heavy to throw. Doyle lifted the Yeti head from his shoulders.

"Hold on a second, Bumble." Tony blinked several times. He raised the gun higher and leveled it at Doyle's face. "Just who the heck are you?"

Chapter 5

"Who am I?" Doyle asked.

"That's what I asked." Tony sneered and waggled the now-silenced gun. "C'mon, Bumble, out with it."

Doyle considered the costume helmet he now held. Maybe these guys weren't after him after all. Perhaps he could get out of this situation with little fuss. He told Tony what he wanted to know. "Doyle Flanders."

"What kind of name is that?"

"What's wrong with it?"

"Sounds like you should be drilling out a cavity."

Doyle's previous identities had run the gamut from the cool to the ridiculous. His first witness inspector had named him Brody Steele, which sounded like an action movie star. Had Doyle known the obstacles he was about to face while in the Witness Protection Program, he might have been a bit more respectful of that alias.

His last witness inspector had the audacity to once base his moniker on her favorite country artist. It was humiliating for a grown man to run around with the name of Skeeter. If the worst thing about his current name was it reminded some two-bit thug of a dentist, Doyle would take it.

"Where's Macklin?" Tony asked.

"Who?"

"The guy who was supposed to be in that costume."

"Porter?"

"That's the name he gave?" Tony scrunched his face. "His name's Macklin. Don't let him fool you."

This misunderstanding was about the theme park's latest hire? What could a low-rent actor have done to warrant the ire of the mob?

Tony jiggled the gun. "Well? Where is he?"

"He went home sick."

"No, he didn't."

Doyle shrugged. "As far as I know, he did. I was told to put on the costume and entertain the kids."

Tony frowned. "Are you his partner?"

"I just work here."

"Doing what?"

"I'm a custodian."

Tony smirked. "No, you're not."

"I pick up trash."

"Likely story. Macklin always works with partners." He waved his gun. "You're his partner."

"You're confusing me with someone else."

"Tell it to the boss, Bumble."

"Can I ask a question?"

Tony started to reach into his pocket but stopped. "It's from *Rudolph the Red-Nosed Reindeer*."

"What is?"

"Bumble. He's the Abominable Snowman. Don't you remember watching that show as a kid?"

Doyle had watched the show with his grandmother but didn't remember anything beyond Rudolph. "That wasn't my question."

Tony studied Doyle. "Make it quick."

"What's with the getup?" Doyle motioned the helmet toward Tony's Hawaiian shirt and shorts. It was a subtle way for him to get a feel for how heavy the head was.

"Think, Bumble, think." Tony tapped the side of his temple with the silenced gun. "We can't exactly move about Fun Time looking like we usually do, now can we?"

"How do you normally look?"

"Are you trying to be smart?"

Doyle hefted the helmet again. "No."

"Well, you're doing a good job of it. We gotta strategize or we'll draw too much attention to ourselves."

Doyle's gaze dropped to the man's black socks and garters.

"That's a regrettable oversight," Tony said. "Our guy forgot the sandals, but what are you gonna do? He won't forget the next time, I'll guarantee that. You get what I'm saying?"

"Yeah," Doyle said. "I get what you're saying."

"Do you? Because there won't be a next time."

"I realize that."

"Don't be playing thick." Tony looked down as he removed his phone from a pocket, then he dialed a number. "It's me," he said. "Yeah, so we got us a problem." Tony rolled his eyes. "Okay, fine. I got a problem, and I'm sorry I said it the way I did. Is that better? Fine. Yeah, I'll wait."

Doyle stopped worrying about his situation. It seemed unlikely Tony would kill him now, since they wanted Porter instead. Or was it Macklin? Either way, Doyle continued to wonder why some local thugs wanted an amusement park actor.

Who were these made guys? Doyle never imagined the mob operated in Lindo Gato, Texas. The Lone Star State seemed an odd place for them to set up. Although maybe they had expanded into new markets. Sort of like soft drink companies did.

Maybe this Macklin fellow borrowed some money and failed to pay it back. If that was the case, Doyle could understand why he had to change his name and why these guys came after the actor. However, this level of response seemed excessive for a man who was behind on his payment schedule—unless this Macklin borrowed a lot.

Doyle's gaze drifted to the disassembled roller coaster cars.

Tony's boss had cleared out the men tearing down The Summit so they would have a quiet area to deal with Macklin. The boss sent armed men inside an occupied theme park to grab the man. Whatever Macklin had done was far worse than failing to pay back some money.

Tony started talking again. "I got the wrong guy. In the monkey suit. Yeah, it's the wrong one. That's what I'm saying. I don't know when they made the switch, but they did. Macklin had to be on to us, right? This guy? It's not one of his regular partners. I don't know, but he looks like a mope."

Doyle cocked his head. He'd been insulted a lot over his life, but no one ever called him a mope, not even the cops.

"You want I should let him go?" Tony joggled the gun at Doyle as he spoke to the caller. "Right. Forget about it. Huh? I already asked him. He doesn't know. All right. I'll ask him again." Tony focused on Doyle. "Where's Macklin?"

"He went home sick."

"Did you hear that? That's right. He said he went home sick." Tony rolled his eyes again. "Yeah, yeah. I'll tell him." Once again, Tony focused on Doyle. "Macklin never left the park. We're watching all the exits, so your partner is still inside."

"He's not my partner. Mr. Gilbert told me to put on the costume, so that's what I did."

"Who's Gilbert?"

"The park manager."

Tony lifted the phone to his mouth. "You get all that? The park manager told him to put it on. That's what I said. I don't think this one involved. He called Macklin by the name Porter. No, Macklin's not a porter. He called him Porter. No, I'm not sure. How can I be sure?" Tony covered the phone's microphone by holding it against his chest. "You better not be jerking my chain with this Macklin thing, or I swear." He bit his lower lip and grunted. Tony lifted the phone back to his ear. "What's that? I should do what? Fine. Yeah. Whatever."

Tony removed the phone from his ear. He awkwardly fiddled with it because of the gun in his other hand. He then lifted it as if he were snapping a photograph. Tony played with the phone some more before returning it to his ear. "You get that?"

"Did you take my picture?" Doyle asked.

Tony heatedly kicked some dirt in Doyle's direction. "Didn't I tell you? The guy's a mope, right?"

"Great," Doyle muttered. "You took my picture."

"You're running that through what?" Tony asked. "Facial recognition? I never heard we had that. When did we get it?"

"Tell me next time," Doyle said. "I'll make sure to smile."

"He's not doing nothing." Tony smirked. "He's literally standing here with his head in his hands."

Doyle hefted the Yeti helmet again. He was getting a pretty good feel for its weight.

"The costume head," Tony said. "Never mind. It was a joke. Fine. I didn't use it correct. I was trying to be funny. What? *Correctly.*" Tony looked toward the sky. "All right. I didn't use literally correctly. Are you happy? Leo? He's outside. Why? Watching for trouble. What do you think he's doing? Don't snap at me. I'll get him inna minute."

Doyle now knew where the second man went. Had he managed to overpower Tony somehow, he would have stepped through the gate and into the waiting arms of Leo.

"What, you got a hit back already? Yeah, I know we got the fast internet, but... you gotta be kidding." Tony's eyes widened, and he leveled the gun at Doyle. "A biker gang? This mope?"

Doyle bent his knees slightly, and the rest of his muscles coiled. He gently bounced the Yeti helmet in his hands.

"He doesn't look like no outlaw," Tony said. "Wait. Do I get a bonus or something for this?" He chuckled. "Oh, for sure. We'll hold him here. What about Macklin? Yeah. Good to know. Okay, see you soon."

Tony ended his call. "A real-life rat," he said. "We have ways of dealing with guys like you in the Outfit."

Doyle's jaw tightened. Now he knew who he was dealing with. He'd heard of them before. It was difficult to run in his world and not hear names like the Outfit. It was a sister group to the mob, much like the Syndicate, the Federation, and the Organization.

For years, the mob wouldn't even acknowledge the existence of these splinter groups. They tried to pass themselves off as being part of the larger entity, but anyone on the inside knew the truth. These groups were flies on the back of the beast—irritating at times but not worth the energy to swat them off. The mob had more lucrative opportunities to focus its energy on.

The media blended these terms in movies and books until they became homogenous. Even Doyle occasionally referred to the mob as the Syndicate or the Outfit, but that was sloppy thinking. Citizens were guilty of the same behavior when they called generic cola drinks Cokes.

Perhaps technology had leveled the playing field for these breakaway associations. What kind of information could the mob hold over their heads if anyone could access everything at the click of a button? Computers weren't Doyle's strong point. If he could imagine something, surely someone smarter would have invented it. The mob kept an online repository for FBI informants, and it sounded as if the Outfit had access to it. Perhaps a thaw had occurred between the mob and the splinter groups.

The world had changed for many industries. Maybe the same had occurred with the mob and it needed alliances more than it needed pride.

Tony leered at him. "It's gonna be a real joy messing up a dirty fink like you." He tried to slip his phone into the pocket of his khaki shorts but missed. He looked down as he repeated the process.

That's when Doyle threw the Abominable Snowman head. He intended to hit Tony in the face but miscalculated the helmet's weight. It dropped quickly and the Yeti head smacked the man's hand. Tony jerked the trigger in surprise. The gun fired a round into the ground with a soft thwip.

Riders on a roller coaster screamed in delight while a calliope played a cheery tune. Somewhere a balloon burst.

Doyle didn't hesitate. He clomped several steps forward and leaped. Tony yelped as he tried to bring the gun up to defend himself. When Doyle hit the man, the weapon continued its path and arced several feet away from them.

Due to the costume, Doyle couldn't make fists inside the gloves, so he mauled Tony like an Abominable Snowman might. Paws viciously rained down on the Outfit man and blood spattered in the shadow of the now silent Summit.

Chapter 6

Doyle Flanders struggled to his feet and looked toward the plywood gate. It was unlikely Leo heard the muffled shot from Tony's gun, but perhaps he had. If Leo came in now, Doyle was too far from the gate to startle the man and he couldn't get to Tony's gun quickly enough to defend himself.

He was a man on an island.

The gate did not open for several impossibly long seconds. During that time, Doyle noticed not only the sounds and smells of the park but a slight breeze was blowing in from the gulf. The wind cooled the sweat on his forehead.

When he was certain Leo wasn't about to burst into the sectioned-off area, Doyle relaxed. He turned his attention to the unconscious Tony. The man's crumpled body looked as if he had tried to twist himself into a smaller mass while Doyle had pummeled him. Tony's face resembled freshly ground hamburger.

Beyond The Summit's plywood walls, a child shrieked with delight. "Cotton candy!"

Doyle removed the Yeti paw from his right hand and tossed it near the costume's helmet. He recovered Tony's gun before plodding over to the plywood fence.

He gently opened the gate. The loud cheers and high-pitched squeals of roller coaster riders flooded in. Merry steam organ music played. A mass of awkward boys followed a group of giggling, skipping teenage girls. The aroma of fried dough and roasted peanuts hovered nearby.

A man roughly Doyle's size stood with his back to the fence. Like the now unconscious Tony, Leo wore khaki shorts and a Hawaiian shirt, although his was garish orange and white. Slouching black socks and scuffed loafers completed his outfit.

Doyle moved behind the gate and softly called, "Hey, Leo."

He had to lure the thug inside—the way a hunter might entice an unsuspecting deer with a salt lick. For many reasons, Doyle didn't want to tangle with Leo on The Pathway of Fun. He was not worried about being filmed or photographed. It no longer mattered if Doyle's picture made it to one of the social media platforms. Tony had photographed him and texted it to someone outside the park. That person ran it through a facial recognition program to see if Doyle was a partner of Porter's. Or was it Macklin? Doyle decided it was the latter.

Doyle's picture was now surely linked to his record on thefbiisabunchofdirtyrats.com. Because of that, the Outfit would likely report Doyle's sighting. The mob wanted him because of the incident with one of their bosses in Maine. The Outfit could curry favor with the big boys by turning him over.

Or perhaps the Outfit called the Satan's Dawgs. They were offering a reward for his capture, or worse.

Maybe the Outfit would keep his sighting to themselves. Doyle had done nothing to the Outfit, but if they suspected him of working with Macklin, they might want some sort of payback. Doyle would like to know what Macklin did to them to get this level of attention.

And yet, maybe there was no choice. Once the Outfit ran his picture through facial recognition, the software might have alerted all those who were interested.

Whatever the outcome, one thing was certain. He looked back at the unconscious Tony. Doyle had now given the Outfit a reason for wanting some payback against him.

None of that mattered. What did was the laughing and smiling families wandering around Lone Star Family Fun Time. Doyle might not like kids—he surely didn't like their parents—but he wouldn't want any of them hurt.

Bracing Leo in the open created a wild-card scenario. The man might pull a gun and fire an errant shot. He could be a professional and consider his surroundings before tugging the trigger or he might be a psychopath and shoot up a crowded theme park, hoping to hit Doyle. There was no way to know.

"Yo, Tony," Leo said. "You called for me?"

Doyle crouched behind the plywood gate and prepared himself. His right hand clutched the silenced gun he'd taken from Tony and his finger teased the trigger. He lifted his left arm in the air—the heavy Yeti glove covered his hand.

"Tony?" Leo's deep voice said just before he poked his head around the edge of the gate. He laughed. "You lying down on the job or something?" His eyes widened as he took in his fallen comrade. They enlarged further as they drifted to the partially costumed Yeti standing right next to him. "What the—"

Doyle violently swatted Leo across the face. "Arrgh!"

Leo screamed before collapsing to the ground like a mushy sack of potatoes.

In retrospect, Doyle knew it was unnecessary to cry out like he did, but the horror in Leo's expression added to the moment's joy.

He dragged the thug through the gate, then closed it.

***

Doyle quickly dismantled the two guns. He threw the pieces and the ammunition in various directions. If Tony or Leo wanted to reassemble their weapons, it would take them a considerable amount of time to find the parts.

Doing that went against his better judgment. The man he used to be would never have done it. But Doyle didn't want the temptation to use a gun while inside Fun Time. He was an excellent shot, but no one was precise enough to guarantee nobody got hurt inside a crowded theme park.

He patted down the two men. Neither had wallets nor any sort of identification. Both had old-style flip phones—the same as he had back in his locker. They were cheap and disposable. Burners. He spun and threw Leo's as far as he could. It clattered against one of The Summit's support girders. Plastic and microchips exploded like a fireworks display.

Tony's phone rang and the caller ID screen illuminated. Doyle threw it as it rang again. It tumbled end-over-end and arced through the crisscrossed girders. The phone eventually landed on compacted dirt and skittered for several feet. It was a disappointing end compared to the explosion of Leo's phone. Doyle trotted over to where he threw it and stomped on it.

Right after he heard the satisfying crunch under the Yeti boot, he realized he made a mistake. His cell phone was in his locker at the administration building. Per Fun Time policy, no employees could have cell phones while on the clock. This was in response to some previous workers chatting, texting, or tweeting when they should have been taking care of the amusement park guests. So the only form of communication employees had was the radios.

This wasn't usually a problem for Doyle since he didn't have anyone to call. Now that his cover was blown, he could have used a telephone.

Doyle didn't find handcuffs or zip-ties on Leo or Tony, so there was no way to secure the men to each other or the roller coaster cars. This gave him pause. They had not expected to take a hostage; they came for revenge. What had Macklin done to the Outfit?

He briefly considered taking Tony and Leo's clothes. However, the Hawaiian shirts and khaki shorts were hideous. Had Doyle been wearing anything underneath the costume, he would simply dump it and run back to the locker room. Trotting barefoot along The Pathway of Fun while wearing only a pair of plaid boxers was not the least conspicuous way to move about the park.

He picked up the Yeti helmet and paw. Doyle had to make one more appearance as Yango. He'd get to his locker, change his clothes, then get out of Lone Star Family Fun Time forever.

Doyle slipped on the helmet and smelled the aroma of stale Fritos once more. He tromped toward the gate and stepped out.

Chapter 7

Doyle pulled the gate closed, flipped over the hasp, and put the lock through the loop. Then he snapped it shut. There was no need for him to get back into The Summit. If the Outfit wanted their men, it would require some extra work and time to get inside the cordoned off area.

He stuck his hand into the Yeti paw and turned around.

"Look who it is," Sophia said. She tugged her daughter closer. "Taylor, say hi."

"No."

Some others from the Seahorse Prep Academy field trip gathered around the mother and daughter. Although the group was considerably smaller now, the mothers in this crowd seemed more excited to see Yango than the kids.

Doyle pointed in the direction of the administration building. "I can't stay."

"He's still talking," Taylor said.

Ezra moved to the front of the group to stand next to the girl. "So unprofessional."

Sophia absently waved off her daughter and the boy. "Don't listen to them. I love what you've done with your costume!"

Several moms pushed past their children.

"Just wonderful," one said. She mimed pawing at him. "Rawr."

"I'm getting the willies," said another mother. "So scary."

Doyle looked down, but the helmet limited his visibility.

"The blood looks so real," Sophia said. She touched the chest of the Yeti costume, then rubbed her fingers together. "And it's on your paws, too!" She laughed with delight. "Oh, I want another picture."

"Me, too," a couple of mothers said in unison. They reached for their phones.

Doyle shimmied to the side. "Really, I can't."

"Still talking," several kids said in unison.

"Wait!" Sophia hollered, but Doyle was running along The Pathway of Fun now.

Although running was an exaggeration. He lumbered as fast as he could toward the administration building, which was on the other side of the park. Doyle lifted the heavy booties and took long, loping strides. His breathing quickly became ragged, and every exhale blew the aroma of stale Fritos back into his face.

The temperature inside the Yeti costume rose, and sweat raced down his back. Doyle tried to look over his shoulder, but whenever he turned his head, all he got was the dark inside of the Yango helmet. After a couple of minutes of tromping, he stopped.

He hunched and put his hands on his knees. Doyle greedily inhaled, then exhaled heavily. The sound coming from the costume must have been horrible. It's then he realized a little boy stood next to him with an ice cream cone. His eyes were wide with fear.

Doyle reached a bloody paw toward him. "Relax, kid. It's okay."

"Him!" the boy screamed. "Not me!"

The kid dropped his cone and ran away.

"Kaden!" a man hollered.

Doyle straightened and came face to face with the boy's father.

"What is it with you people? I just calmed him down after that darn raccoon wound him up." The father hurried after his boy.

"Making friends, I see."

Doyle turned around.

Oskar VanLeuven exited a golf cart with two trash cans on the back. He managed the Fun Time custodial crew. He was a lean man in his early sixties. Oskar had worked at the park since leaving high school. From his earliest days, he'd been on the clean-up crew. Oskar had told Doyle he never aspired to do anything different. "Why for?" he had said. "Fun Time is the greatest place on earth. It's nothing but good times and smiles. Nothing bad ever happens here."

Doyle waved a bloody paw in the direction the boy ran. "The kid doesn't like the costumes."

"Neither do I. Bunch of prima donnas inside them if you ask me, and here you go being one. I had high hopes for you, Flanders."

Doyle had never thought of himself as a diva. His already sour mood worsened. "You need something? I'm on my way toward the locker room."

"I'll walk with you."

"What about your cart?"

"I'll come back for it." Oskar motioned at the park's customers. "Besides, who would steal it?"

"I meant you could give me a ride."

"And miss the opportunity for a walk?"

Oskar reached up and patted Doyle's shoulder. Oskar stood more than a foot shorter than Doyle and might have been seventy-five pounds lighter. The two men headed toward the administration building.

Doyle scanned the crowd for anyone who might look like they worked with Tony or Leo. He figured men in the Outfit might be dressed in one of two ways. They could wear those absurd Hawaiian shirts like Tony and Leo did. However, Doyle had yet to see anyone else wearing a shirt that reminded him of *Magnum P.I.*, the show his grandmother used to love.

If an Outfit man wasn't dressed like that fictional detective, Doyle thought they might wear a suit. The dark socks and shoes Tony and Leo wore pointed him in that direction. Otherwise, they wouldn't have needed a disguise. Again, he didn't notice anyone dressed in that manner.

While moving through the crowd with Oskar, several parents eyed Doyle with concern. Many children stared at him with open wonderment. All the attention bugged him.

"Arrgh!"

Two little girls screamed. Their mothers gathered the children in and glared at Doyle.

"Tone it down, why don't ya?" Oskar said.

Doyle immediately felt bad. "Sorry," he said to the kids. He looked at their mothers. "I'm new to this."

Oskar motioned toward Doyle's chest. "Looks like some brat threw a slushie on you."

Doyle lifted his hands in front of his face. Blood covered the left paw. There was some on the right. Tony and Leo's blood must have been all over the costume.

"It's a heck of an improvement if you ask me," Oskar said. "Maybe we should smear some of that slush on the mouth. You'd be a real fright then." He cackled. "Although, that sort of defeats the idea of being the funnest place in Lindo Gato, doesn't it?"

Doyle continued to scan the mass of people. Still no Hawaiian shirts or dark suits. But he saw someone he knew headed his way.

The big man was roughly Doyle's size. He wore a yellow Fun Time sweatshirt, dark slacks, and loafers. He carried a large gym bag over his shoulder. The big man stopped walking when he recognized Doyle.

More likely, the big man noticed the Abominable Snowman costume. Whatever it was, the big guy stopped and looked about before disappearing into a mass of people.

"Where the heck did he go?" Doyle muttered.

Oskar's head swiveled. "Where did *who* go?"

"Macklin."

"Who?"

Doyle waved a paw. "I mean, Porter."

"He went home sick. You know that." The custodial boss put his hands on his hips as he scanned the nearby crowd. "But if he's feeling better, let's get you out of that stupid costume and back to doing an honest day's worth of work."

Doyle moved to the right.

"Where you going?" Oskar asked. "We were talking."

He didn't answer. He was searching for his quarry. Macklin had somehow blended into a group full of parents and children. It confused Doyle.

"Hey, listen," Oskar said. "Ol' Gilbert can't hijack my crew whenever he wants just because he's short a furry. We all got responsibilities."

Doyle plodded forward. The heavy booties slapped the asphalt, and his breathing quickly grew ragged again. Every exhale forced the stale Frito stink to blow back into his face.

"Come back here, you!" Oskar hollered.

But Doyle didn't. He continued to follow the mass of people until they arrived at Lucky's Alley. The group of families dispersed among various games of chance with names like The Ring Toss, Skee-Ball, Bust-a-Balloon, Milk Bottle Knockdown, and High Striker.

Soon no one stood in the middle of the alley except Doyle.

Macklin had vanished.

Doyle raised his arms in the air. "Arrgh!"

Nearby, a little boy shrieked, and a mother said, "You monster!"

"Give it a rest," Oskar rasped. He ran in front of Doyle. The supervisor was about to say something further, but he inhaled deeply instead. He lifted a hand as if to tell Doyle to wait. Oskar bent over and gulped for air. He snapped his fingers several times and pointed at Doyle. When he got himself under control, he looked up. "Well? Was that Porter or not?"

"I think so."

Oskar pushed himself upright. "You think so? What good is that going to do us? I can't go to Gilbert with you only thinking so." His head bobbled side to side. "Then again, I guess I could. That's probably good enough. So you saw him?"

Doyle shrugged, which was tough in the costume.

"Heck, that's good enough for me. I'm gonna make a stink about this. I wanna get you back on the crew."

How had Macklin slipped away in a crowd of families? Doyle had his eye on him the whole time. It's like the yellow sweatshirt was there one moment and then not. Doyle spun around until he spotted a trash can. He hurried over to it and looked inside. Laying on top was a yellow sweatshirt.

Oskar followed him over. "Unless you like wearing that silly get up which is okay, I guess. You know they got conventions for people like you. Furries, they call them. Not that there's anything wrong with it. Lifestyle choices and all. I just never figured you to be one of them types, Flanders."

Had Macklin planned ahead with the sweatshirt, or was it a fortunate choice of clothing? Doyle had to assume he chose the outerwear with the purpose of ditching it if needed. If that was the case, was being sick just a scam? If his illness was a fraud, why did he need the job at Family Fun Time if he was going to be sick on his first day? Did he get hired to get access to the park for one day? Wouldn't it have been easier to buy a day pass? What would being an employee give him that being a customer would not?

Doyle's mind flew through the possibilities. Certainly restricted access to areas of the park. Maybe a key card. There were too many areas of the park guests couldn't go. So what was it?

"Well," Oskar said, "if dressing up in a furry costume makes you happy, I won't stand in your way. Although, I did sort of hire you with the expectation you would do a job, so maybe you can pick up some trash while you're walking around here expressing your inner snowman."

If Macklin planned some sort of job at Fun Time, what was he after? Was that the reason the Outfit wanted him?

So many thoughts raced through Doyle's head that he couldn't keep them straight. He turned and headed toward the administration building.

"Good talk, Flanders," Oskar hollered. "Always a pleasure!"

Doyle absently held up a bloody paw as he continued to wander away.

***

"Hey!" a thick, male voice called. "Hey, bro!"

Doyle hunched, prepared to fight. He scanned left and right for Hawaiian shirts or dark suits, but none registered.

However, Sassy Sasquatch bounded over. He waved his brown, furry paws as he ran.

Doyle relaxed. Even though he didn't often mingle with the actors inside the costumes, he occasionally bumped into them. He'd met the man responsible for playing Sassy Sasquatch in the administration building's lunchroom. Doyle didn't know the actor's real name, but the guy had introduced himself as Zeus. "As in the god of surf, you know?" he said mystically.

Outside the costume, Zeus had long, golden hair and a deep tan, even though it was winter. He was slightly shorter than Doyle and quite a bit leaner. When he wasn't working on his acting chops as Sassy Sasquatch, Zeus was riding the surf along the Lindo Gato beaches.

"Whoa, broseph!" Zeus said as he neared. "I've been looking for you."

Doyle glanced around. He didn't like the optics of Bigfoot and the Abominable Snowman meeting in the middle of Fun Time. It was bound to attract a crowd.

"Make it quick, Zeus. I've got to run."

"You look good as the abomina-bro snowman." He grabbed Doyle's arms and turned him side to side. "You sure you haven't acted before?"

Doyle felt a strange burst of pride, but he fought it back. While in Wyoming recently, he wondered if he might have been capable of starring in a high school play. It was something he had never considered before.

Guests snapped photographs of the two mascots now.

"Like you should come to my acting class," Zeus said. "We're working on non-verbal, spatial awareness. It's radically enlightening stuff." He put his paws to his head, then moved them quickly away. "Kablooey! Like totally mind-blowing, brohizzle."

"Thanks for the invitation, but I've got somewhere to be." Doyle pointed toward the administration building. "Was there something important?"

"Whoa!" Zeus said. He carried the word into multiple syllables. "Slow down, broham. I love what you did with the costume. Is that ketchup?" Zeus rubbed his paw on Doyle's chest. "Can I get some of that?"

"Why were you looking for me?"

Now, Zeus dragged his paw over the tangled brown fur of his own costume. "Why's this ketchup not showing up?"

"Zeus."

The guy aggressively rubbed his paw on his costume. "Maybe the sauce is already dry."

A larger crowd gathered to photograph the two men. Some were even taking selfies.

"*Zeus*," Doyle said.

"Huh?"

"Why were you looking for me?"

He chuckled. "Oh, right." He clapped his paws several times. "Mr. Gilbert wants you back at The Terror."

Doyle turned toward the administration building.

Zeus grabbed Doyle's arm. "Wrong way, bro." He pointed in the opposite direction. "It's that-a-way."

"Why don't you go for me?"

"I'm on break, broski. An artist needs time to clear his mind, you know? To reset his internal peace and align his chakra."

"Well, there you go." Doyle yanked his arm free as he searched for Outfit men. "I'm on my break, too."

"We can't go on break at the same time!" Zeus bent his knees and thrust his paws toward Fun Time's latest ride. "There are kids waiting at The Terror for you. Be like Han Brolo and save them from the Empire of Boredom."

"I'll pass."

Zeus patted his furry chest with both paws. "But this is my break time."

"All right," Doyle said. "Leaving now." He walked away.

"C'mon, bromeister!" Zeus hollered. "You're harshing my mellow."

Doyle had only walked a couple of steps when he stopped suddenly.

Fifty yards away were three men dressed like Tony and Leo—gaudy Hawaiian shirts, khaki shorts, and black loafers. One held an unfolded park map while the others pointed at it. None of the men noticed Doyle, but they were headed in his direction.

Overhead, a speaker crackled. "*Welcome Family Fun Time visitors! Have you grabbed your officially licensed Yango the Yeti merchandise yet? If not, stop at any of our conveniently located shops to buy an assortment of trinkets. We have T-shirts, coffee mugs, keychains, and more. Grab something to commemorate your day with Yango!*"

Doyle turned to leave, but two teenagers blocked his escape. Both had their cell phones out.

"Nice!" the bigger one said with a stretched out chuckle. He had long greasy hair, a pimply face, and a T-shirt that read *A Nightmare on Elm Street* above an image of a scar-faced man. "Get my picture, dude. This Yeti looks just like the one from *Bloodbath in the Alps*." He moved toward Doyle.

His friend had cleaner hair and a less irritated face. His black T-shirt read *Halloween* above an image of a hand holding a knife. "Is that the one where the girl dies after the

Abominable Snowman impales her with her own ski?"

"That's the one." The bigger teenager grabbed Doyle's arm and put it around his neck. "How's this look?"

Doyle cranked the teenager into a headlock and pulled him down to his waist. "Not now."

"Aw, man," the smaller one exclaimed. "That's great! Hold on for a sec."

The bigger teenager frantically slapped Doyle's arm. "Can't breathe," he squeaked.

Doyle released him and the teenager fell to the ground.

He looked up at his friend. "Tell me you got that picture!"

"It's all blurry," the second one said. "Hey, Mr. Yeti, sir? Can we get another picture?"

"No," Doyle said. He stepped away from the teenagers.

The bigger one said, "Let's get the Sasquatch!"

The two boys took off after Zeus.

The three men in Hawaiian shirts hurried by. One pointed ahead in the general direction of The Summit. They must be the reinforcements that Tony had requested.

Someone touched Doyle's shoulder. He spun and lifted his arm in the air, prepared to strike.

"Take it easy, tough guy," security guard Ainsley Sutherland said. She beamed. "You're really getting into this Abominable Snowman gig, aren't you?"

Doyle dropped his hand. He had focused so much on the Outfit's men that he hadn't heard her golf cart zip up. It was parked behind her. He turned around to watch the three men in Hawaiian shirts, but they had disappeared into a crowd of families.

Ainsley stepped in front of him and inspected the chest of his costume. "Is that blood? How'd you make that look so real?"

He backpedaled. "No time."

"Hold on, mister."

"I can't."

"Something's going on around here."

Doyle paused. The Yeti costume was unbearably hot then and sweat dripped from his armpits. Part of the perspiration was caused by his running, but the other part had to be from the adrenaline coursing through his veins. He wanted to get out of the costume and into some cooler clothes. Pretty soon, those Outfit guys were going to realize he overwhelmed Tony and Leo and go searching for a Yeti.

"What do you think's going on?" he asked.

Ainsley glanced over her shoulder. "Did you see those guys in Hawaiian shirts? What's up with that? Is there some sort of convention going on in town? Grumpy old guys never come here without their families." She motioned about Fun Time. "Also, there are dark cars parked outside every exit. The ticket cashiers radioed me about them, so I went and scoped it out. They're right. All their windows were blacked out—at least, the cars I saw at the exits I checked. The whole setup is sort of menacing if you ask me."

Fun Time had one entrance and three emergency exits. It wouldn't take many men to cover those. Four roads ran parallel to the park. Could the Outfit have a roving car to make sure he or Macklin didn't hop a fence?

"What do you make of it?" Doyle had a good idea but wanted to hear what she had to say.

Ainsley shrugged. "I asked Mr. Gilbert, but he told me not to worry about it."

"He did?" That surprised Doyle.

She continued. "If I was running this place and there were a bunch of creepy dudes parked at all the exits, I think I would worry about it."

"How do you know they're men?"

Ainsley frowned. "You think a bunch of women would park like that at the exits and do nothing? Hello? That's a total dude idea. Trust me." She shook her head. "No. If those were women, they'd be outside those cars, yelling and pointing at whoever they were mad at to get their worthless you-know-whats out of Fun Time so they could talk. They'd make such a big stink that everyone would know what was going on. At least, that's what I think they would do."

Doyle had never considered what would happen if a group like the Outfit suddenly became all female. Not that it couldn't happen in an upside-down bizarro world. In Doyle's experience, women were simply smarter and nicer than men. They tended not to get involved in the pursuit of violent stupidity like Doyle's gender.

So was Mr. Gilbert involved with the Outfit? Or did they have him over a barrel?

Ainsley stood on her tiptoes to peer into the mouth of the Yeti costume. "Are you awake in there? And something else, did you notice how the crew taking down The Summit walked off the job this morning?"

"I did."

"Gilbert told me to leave that alone, too."

"Probably good advice," Doyle said.

Ainsley inhaled sharply and put her hands on her hips. "Not you, too?"

The Outfit's men had brought guns into a theme park, and they grabbed him. It communicated everything he needed to know about what they were willing to do. He liked Ainsley and didn't want her to get hurt.

Doyle wanted to scan for new threats, but the Yango helmet limited his visibility. He wanted to pull the darn head off so he could freely look about but doing so would call even more attention to himself. Better to stay in costume a little while longer. Once he could ditch the Yeti gear, everything would be fine.

"Listen," Doyle said, "I've gotta go. Listen to what Gilbert told you and leave it alone."

She grabbed his paws and stood on her tiptoes to look at him in the Yeti's maw. "Do you know what's going on?"

"Steer clear of the guys in Hawaiian shirts."

"Why?" Ainsley's face reddened. "What kind of conference are they attending? I'm the head of security. Tell me what's happening."

"There are plans you and your team won't be able to deal with."

She stepped back and put her hands on her hips again. "I'll have you know I can handle a lot. So what if it's just me and the goofballs today? We've handled worse than some badly dressed conventioneers."

"That's not what this is."

"It's not?" Ainsley cocked her head. "Then what is it? Should we call the cops?"

"No." Doyle liked cops about as much as he liked thugs from The Outfit.

Ainsley's walkie-talkie crackled. *"Sutherland, this is Gilbert. Have you seen the Yeti?"*

Doyle shook his head, but it didn't move the Abominable Snowman helmet. "Tell him no."

Her expression hardened as she tugged the radio from her belt. "Yes, sir. I'm looking at him right now. Is there something you'd like me to tell him?"

"Have him report immediately to the administration building." Gilbert's voice sounded strained.

Doyle stiffened.

"Yes, sir." Ainsley nodded. "Will do."

He pointed at the walkie-talkie. "Ask him why he wants me to report in."

"No," Ainsley said. She clipped the radio back to her belt.

"Why not?"

"Because he's the boss." Her expression hardened. "As you said, you do what he tells you to do."

Ainsley climbed into her golf cart and zipped away.

Chapter 8

Sweat rolled down Doyle's back. Had he been in his custodian uniform—a tan shirt and brown pants—the temperature might have made for a nice, comfortable day. He might even have worn a light jacket.

However, slogging around Family Fun Time in the Yeti costume was harder work than he expected. He paused briefly to think maybe he should give the actors more credit for the work they did. Not only did they have to wear the weighty costumes, but they also had to deal with kids and families.

Doyle needed a new plan. Mr. Gilbert's order for him to return to the administration building spelled trouble. Either Gilbert was colluding with the Outfit, or he was under their influence. Either way, his order meant the Outfit knew Doyle had escaped from Tony and Leo and was running around free in Fun Time now. He had to ditch this costume fast.

The trouble was his clothes, apartment key, and cell phone were in his locker. Each represented a unique problem. He needed the clothes once he slipped out of the Yango getup. The key was necessary to return home and get his cat. Of the three, the cell phone was probably the least important. It didn't have any numbers saved in it. He had memorized the emergency number Marshal Krumland had given him.

Doyle needed to find a phone. The administration building had them, of course. He wasn't sure if the Fun Time stores had them since he always saw employees communicating via radios. He knew he could find one, though. If push came to shove, he'd borrow one from a guest.

He trotted along The Pathway of Fun. He didn't know where he was going but being in motion felt good. He feared standing still. The heavy booties clomped with each step. He felt lightheaded as the temperature continued to rise in the costume.

Ahead, a few families in lines for various rides and merchandise shops turned to watch Doyle run by. Several parents pulled younger children back as they reached out to him. The ever-present calliope music added a strange soundtrack to the moment.

A smiling boy struggled to get free from his mother's clutches. As Doyle ran past, the kid lifted his fist into the air. "Go, Yango, go!"

Several children giggled behind him. Doyle couldn't see over his shoulder because of the helmet's limited visibility. He slowed and turned.

A gaggle of kids looked expectantly at him. They all appeared to be five and six years old. The children hopped with excitement.

"Yango!" they cheered.

A group of winded parents stood behind them. Many of the adults bent with their hands on their knees. None of them made any moves to corral their kids.

The nearest boy wore a crisp white *I Survived the Terror* T-shirt over a long-sleeved shirt. "Where are we going, Yango?"

A nearby girl bounced, twisted, and sang, "We're going with Yango!"

Doyle glanced around. He didn't see any men in Hawaiian shirts or suits. He needed to get rid of these kids quickly and get on his way. Doyle lifted his arms in the air and towered over the assembled children. "Arrgh!"

The littlest girl in the group squeaked, but the boy closest to her smirked. "That's my sister. She's afraid of everything."

Doyle growled louder and waved his arms like an angry gorilla. That action only brought wider smiles from the assembled children—even the littlest girl now seemed less afraid.

A boy pointed at Doyle's chest. "Look at the blood!"

The other children clamored to get closer.

"Do it again," one girl demanded. She bared her teeth, lifted her arms into the air, and shook her head. Her blond hair flopped from side to side. "Rawr!"

"Yeah!" a boy exclaimed. He now danced like a monkey. "Rawr!"

All the children lifted their arms and ferociously growled. The dancing girl twirled as she snarled and shook her hands in the air.

Doyle's gaze returned to the parents. Most of them had recovered their breath and had straightened. Yet they remained in a weird limbo state. Their eyes had glossed over, and they lifted their phones to take photos. They seemed like obedient servants to their children.

He opened his arms in a questioning manner. "A little help?" He cocked his head and raised his eyebrows, but the effects were lost behind the Yeti helmet.

The parents stared at Doyle in that stupid way they're apt to do when their children are involved. He'd observed similar behavior up-close while working as a mall Santa. Right now, several of the adults squatted and held their cameras at odd angles. Some seemed to consider the position of the sun. One mother implored her daughter to make her roar "more convincing, honey. Really put your soul in to it."

Doyle's lip curled. The jumping and growling children surrounded him now. Scaring these children wasn't working. He needed a different tack.

He flicked his paws. "Go on. Get."

"Huh?" the kid with The Terror T-shirt asked.

"I'm on my lunch break," Doyle said.

"What are you having?" the littlest girl asked.

A blond-haired boy asked, "Do you get to eat funnel cakes every day?" He danced a happy jig. "I'd eat them every day if I lived here."

"Or ice cream?" The twirling girl stopped mid-spin. "Do Yeti's get ice cream for their birthdays?"

The boy with The Terror T-shirt wasn't buying any of it, though. His eyes narrowed, and he pointed an accusatory finger. "Yetis don't get lunch breaks."

"I'm Yango," Doyle said, "and I get a lunch break." He had made a lot of stupid comments over the past few months, but that may have been the dumbest.

"What are you really doing?" the boy in The Terror shirt asked. "You're doing something naughty."

Doyle looked at the parents again, but they were introducing themselves to each other and sharing the photos on their phones. Somehow, he'd found himself in the role of an impromptu babysitter.

"Just stay here," Doyle said. "I gotta go."

The once-twirling girl asked, "Number two?" She made some gesture with her fists that Doyle didn't understand.

"What?"

The blond-haired boy smiled. "To the bathroom."

"No," Doyle said. "Stay here."

"Where's your family?" the littlest girl asked. "Did you run away?"

All the children watched him with wide eyes now. They looked like members of a support group waiting for him to share a pivotal life memory. Doyle was now certain a prison sentence was better than any conversation with a group of children.

Behind the kids, a man in a Hawaiian shirt noticed Doyle and hollered. "The Yeti!" He lumbered in the group's direction.

"Stay," Doyle said. He ran away from the approaching man.

"The bathrooms are the other way!" several children yelled.

Doyle's heavy breathing and clomping boots drowned out the other sounds of the park.

Up ahead was the slowly turning carousel. Riders of all ages went up and down on the forever-frozen horses. Some waved as he stomped by.

The operator shouted, "Looking good, Yango!" but Doyle didn't have time to reply.

He ran behind a row of concession stands and waited. He couldn't outrun the Outfit's man for very long. He knew he had to stop and fight. The thug likely had a gun. The only things Doyle had in his favor were the heavy Yango paws. He raised them in the air.

Up ahead, some riders on the carousel waved at him. A portion of the ride could see behind the concession stands.

Before Doyle could consider a change in plans, the Outfit's man stepped around the corner with a revolver in his hand.

Doyle brought one paw down and smacked the gun free. Then the other slapped the thug across the face. When the man fell, Doyle jumped and straddled his chest. Doyle knew how to fight, but he didn't land a single jab, cross, or uppercut. Instead, he repeatedly slapped the thug across the face with the heavy paws until the thug slipped into unconsciousness.

To an outsider, it must have looked like a mauling. Doyle broke the man's nose and cut his lips. The Outfit's man would certainly have two black eyes. Blood was everywhere. Doyle stood.

Ahead, the carousel continued to spin. Horrified children and adults watched as cheerful calliope music played.

Doyle thought about roaring, but that might further scar the kids. He considered taking a bow and announcing the whole fight was an act. But the guy on the ground wasn't moving. The children would surely know it wasn't true.

In the end, he did the one thing he could.

He ran.

Chapter 9

Doyle had to get out of the Yeti costume fast. It was certainly attracting the wrong kind of attention now. Then again, ever since he entered the Witness Protection Program, Doyle had discovered there was no right kind of attention.

He still wanted to go to the administration building to check on Mr. Gilbert. If the Outfit had pressured him, it was because of Macklin. The man Doyle had been previously would not worry about a guy like the park manager. He would have simply saved his own skin by slipping out of the park any way he could, but that's not who Doyle wanted to be.

If Gilbert was in on the plan with the Outfit, then so be it. He could leave with no further worries. If Gilbert was being held against his will, that changed the situation. Doyle would have to do something about it.

Doyle hurried into Wonder Alley, the part of Fun Time designated for the littlest kids and immediately knew it was a poor decision. The area featured rides and games for toddlers. Included were the Whirling Cups of Wonder, Fun Time's House of Wonder, the Viking Ship to Wonder's Shore, and the mini-Ferris Wheel. Much like the park's original planners, Doyle also couldn't figure out how to put any wonder into a mini-Ferris Wheel.

A cluster of children and parents gathered around Ricky the Raccoon. They laughed and took photographs with the creepy mascot. Freddy the Frog leaned a shoulder against a flagpole. He watched Doyle run by but made no motion toward acknowledgment.

Wandering parents and unbalanced toddlers clogged this strip of the park. Many turned and stared in bewilderment when Doyle thudded into their vicinity. Several children pointed at him.

One overly protective mother covered her child's eyes and cried, "Why? He's just a baby!"

Doyle wondered if it was because of the Abominable Snowman costume or because of the blood splashed across its chest and paws. Perhaps it was both. He waved apologetically at the woman and continued.

He didn't see any Hawaiian shirts or suits. Perhaps he was wrong to assume other Outfit men might be dressed that second way, but Doyle thought it better to be cautious.

The park's speaker hissed before an announcement. *"Welcome to Family Fun Time, the Lone Star state's last independently owned amusement park located here in beautiful Lindo Gato! Have you experienced The Terror yet? Be one of the first and earn your commemorative T-shirt. Wait times may vary."*

A custodian Doyle knew as Shiloh pushed a gray cart overloaded with garbage bags. She looked up and motioned for him to come closer.

He planned to ignore her and hurry by, but Shiloh called out, "Doyle! I know you saw me."

He slowed and approached her.

She was in her early fifties. Her tan and brown uniform hung loosely from her wiry frame. She had gray skin and the raspy voice of a lifetime smoker. "Gilbert's looking for you."

"I know. Pretend you didn't see me."

"Don't drag me down with whatever you're into." She flicked her hand. "Getting in good with the costumes doesn't sway me."

"Cut me a break, Shiloh. I'm one of the crew."

"A break?" She clucked her tongue. "You're traipsing around in those fancy duds without a care in the world while the rest of us are shagging garbage. You're not a part of the crew anymore, thank you very much." She reached for the radio clipped to the side of the cart. "You get what you get."

"Wait." Doyle held out his paws. "I'll go see Gilbert right now." He had no intention of doing so.

Shiloh grunted. "I don't believe you." She lifted the radio to her lips.

"All right, but don't tell him where I am."

Her eyes narrowed. "Why would I do that?"

"Because I'm asking."

"Not good enough." She pressed the transmit button. "Mr. Gilbert, this is Shiloh."

"*This is Gilbert. Who is this?*"

"Shiloh. From the clean-up crew, sir."

"*Oh, yes. What is it?*"

She held the radio next to her mouth but didn't transmit. Her eyes narrowed as she studied Doyle. "Care to try again?"

"What do you want?" Doyle asked.

"*Hello? Shiloh?*"

She motioned toward her cart full of garbage bags. "Finish my rounds, then dump the cart. If you'll do that, I'll tell him I didn't see you."

Doyle couldn't risk the additional time in the costume. Even standing there talking to Shiloh put him at further risk of being seen by the Outfit. He needed to get moving. "I can't," he said. "I'm in the middle of something."

"If that's the way you want to play it." Shiloh pressed the transmit button. "I spoke with Doyle, sir."

"*You did? Oh, well. Okay. Um, where is he?*"

"Fine," Doyle blurted. He patted the air with his paws. "I'll finish your rounds."

"And dump the cart? Don't forget that."

"Yeah, yeah."

It was a lie, of course. Doyle had no plans to finish her rounds, but he didn't want her to report his location to Mr. Gilbert. Doyle didn't want to lie to Shiloh or anyone else for that matter. Doing so went against his desire to be better. However, he didn't see a solution at that moment, except maybe smacking Shiloh and taking her walkie-talkie. That seemed far more harmful to his goal of being better than uttering the lie.

Shiloh lifted the radio to her lips but didn't press the transmit the button. "You promise?"

Doyle's lip curled underneath the Yeti helmet. "I promise."

She pressed the transmit button. "Doyle's on his way to see you."

"*Where did you see him?*"

She cocked her head. "Where did I see you?"

"Lucky's Alley," Doyle said.

"Lucky's Alley," she parroted into the radio.

"*He's back there?*" Gilbert said. "*But they got reports he left.*"

"Who's they?" Shiloh asked Doyle.

He motioned toward the radio.

"Yeah, yeah." She pressed the transmit button. "Don't know what to say, sir, except you can stop worrying. He's headed toward you now."

"*Okay, fine.*"

"Thank you," Doyle said.

Shiloh pointed at the cart of garbage. "Your chariot awaits. I'm going on break now. Leave the cart near the entrance to Wonder Alley, and I'll pick it up there." She clipped the radio to her hip and wandered off. "Smell ya later, Yango."

Doyle put his paws on the cart. He waited several moments until she stepped out of sight, then he abandoned it.

He hurried into a nearby Happy Hour Shop, one of several Fun Time stores around the theme park. There were also Delighted Minute Diners and Ecstatic Seconds Confectionaries to keep attendees fueled up for a full day of excitement. A brass bell rang upon his entry.

Several of the customers in the store stopped browsing to watch Doyle. A little girl reached out to feel his paw, but her father jerked the kid away.

"Mustn't touch," the father said. He waggled a finger in front of the girl's face.

As Doyle walked by the cashier, the woman didn't bother to look away from whatever she was reading. "Can I help you find anything, sir?" she said mechanically.

Doyle stopped in front of her.

Tabitha was in her early twenties with jet-black hair. Her heavy eyeliner clashed with the tan and brown uniform all Fun Time employees wore. *Evil* was tattooed across the back of her right fingers and *grrl* adorned the left digits. When she glanced up and saw the Yeti costume, Tabitha muttered, "Nerts."

"You all right?"

"This job." Her eyelids drooped. "I heard you got drafted today. How do you like being famous?"

"I like trash better." Doyle pointed toward the back of the store. "I need to grab something."

"Help yourself. I like what you did with the costume, by the way. The blood really gives it some oomph."

Doyle went to the promo rack. He slipped off a paw before grabbing a white, extra-large *I Survived the Terror* T-shirt. He moved to the clothing section with hopes of finding a pair of pants, but there were none. Not even a lousy pair of sweats. Reluctantly, he snagged some blue shorts with a Lone Star Family Fun Time logo on its right leg. He looked around for a moment but didn't see any type of footwear. The shirt and shorts would have to do.

There was no dressing room, so Doyle hurried toward the stockroom and opened the door.

"You can't go back there, sir," Tabitha called.

He turned around to look at her.

"Nerts," she said. "Habit." Tabitha waved him on.

Doyle closed the door behind him. The stockroom was full of boxes and shelves. There was an exit out the back of the store. There were no chairs or other places to sit.

He removed the second paw and tossed them both into the corner. Next, he removed the Yeti helmet and threw it as well. Getting a breath of clean air never smelled so wonderful. Over the following handful of seconds, Doyle stripped off the bulky Yeti costume. It all ended up in a pile in the storeroom.

He slipped on the T-shirt and shorts, but remained barefoot. There was a strict No Shirt—No Shoes—No Service policy at Fun Time, but that was the least of his worries. Doyle was concerned about running on the asphalted Pathway of Fun and stepping on something that might cut his foot. He grabbed the hairy Yeti feet and slipped them on.

Doyle considered his appearance. His feet were covered, but the boots were heavy. He would have trouble moving quickly, but it wasn't as bad as before. Now, he looked like a weirdo, which wasn't cool. He had mostly stopped worrying about being stylish months ago.

When he entered the Witness Protection Program, Doyle had to cut his long mane of hair and shave his thick beard. For a time, he even wore khakis and a plaid shirt. But this might have been the lowest level of uncool he had reached. There was no way he was adding a pair of unsightly Yeti feet to an amusement park T-shirt and a pair of blue athletic shorts. He would risk stepping on a pebble.

He pulled the booties off and exited the room.

None of the customers paid him any attention as he moved through the store.

Tabitha, however, did. Her eyebrows lifted and an appreciative smile spread across her lips. "Nice tattoos."

The inky ball of fire on his right hand turned into a snake that ran up his arm and disappeared under his T-shirt. He usually wore a long-sleeved shirt, so the ink was never seen by anyone at work.

"Thanks," he muttered and moved toward the door.

"What happened to Yango?" Tabitha asked.

"I dropped him in the backroom." Doyle glanced through the store windows. He didn't see any Hawaiian shirts.

"Mind if I ask why?"

Doyle had already lied to Shiloh. He didn't want to do it again, so he returned to the counter. He lowered his voice. "I'm trying to avoid Gilbert."

"But he knows what you look like."

"He's looking for Yango." As soon as the words left his mouth, Doyle realized how stupid his excuse sounded. He started to come up with another reason for his actions, but he couldn't find one.

Tabitha lifted a hand. "Don't worry about it. We all hate the costumes. I'm just glad you saw the light and ditched it."

Doyle pulled the hem of his T-shirt. "I'll pay you for these later."

"Before the end of the day," Shiloh said, "or I'll have to come looking for you." She leaned over the counter. "Where are your shoes? You know the park's policy."

"It'll be fine."

Tabitha shrugged. "If you say so."

"Do you have a phone I can use?"

She shook her head. "Fun Time rules. I've already been written up once for sneaking my cell phone back here. Not going to let that happen again."

"What about your landline?"

Tabitha looked below the counter. "No outside calls. You know how it is."

Doyle was about to ask if that included the police, but he was still hesitant to call them. He might be changing his ways, but that didn't mean he wanted the boys in blue getting involved in his business. Besides, the Outfit wasn't looking to hurt anyone at Fun Time. They were only after Macklin and him.

"All right," Doyle said with a nod. He opened the door.

"Have a nice day."

He glanced back.

"Nerts." Tabitha's face pinched. "This job."

When he stepped out of the store, Doyle surveyed Wonder Alley. Parents and children roamed about. The smiles and amazed looks were still on their faces. Now that he was out of the Yango costume, the kids didn't pay him any attention.

Some parents did, however.

A handful of fathers cast disdainful glances at his bare feet or the tattoos which adorned his arms. Several mothers shied away, as if afraid of getting too close to a caged tiger. There were a couple of women, however, who smiled at Doyle while hiding behind the safety of their husbands.

He tugged at the edges of his shorts. Doyle felt silly wearing them—like a little kid. He thought men looked ridiculous in shorts. It was as if they were trying to avoid manhood by dressing like boys. They could hide their Peter Pan issues with names like sports, cargo, or dress, but those men simply didn't want to grow up. Doyle hadn't worn a pair of shorts since he was in high school gym, and he skipped that class half the time to cause trouble in his jeans and black T-shirts.

Doyle searched the crowd for Outfit thugs. He noticed Shiloh's cart full of trash bags and considered running it to the dumpster so he wouldn't have lied to her, but Doyle had bigger issues.

He wanted to get to the administration building and check on Mr. Gilbert. Depending on the outcome, he would adjust his plan. Either he would save himself or he would help Gilbert get free of the Outfit.

After a last glance around, he turned and ran.

And immediately stepped on a pebble.

Doyle grabbed his injured foot and hopped on the other. He wanted to swear, but that was something he never did. He set his foot back down and steeled himself for more sharp little rocks. He hurried now and was far more aware of what was on the ground.

That was the price for looking cool.

***

A golf cart zoomed next to Doyle as he hurried along. Two security guards named Flint and Artie watched him. They were trim, white men in their early twenties. Both had long, wavy hair and tanned skin. Their eyes always seemed on the verge of sleep. They looked as if they could have been part of Zeus's surfing crew.

Flint sat in the passenger seat—the one closest to Doyle. "Yo, dude," he said. "No running. It's like dangerous to the public safety and stuff."

Doyle didn't slow. "Flint, it's me."

Flint pulled back and looked down the bridge of his nose. "Dude! It's you!"

Artie leaned forward and rested his arms on the steering wheel. "Hey, Doyle. Why are you running?"

"I'm in a hurry."

"Makes sense."

The golf cart hit a trash can and Doyle jumped to the side. The can was tethered to a light pole, so it only spun around and didn't fly away, but the racket was horrible. Families stopped to see what was occurring. The cart continued as if nothing had been in its way.

Doyle tried to regain his pace.

"Nice threads," Artie said. He jerked the golf cart to avoid hitting a Fun Time vendor with a handful of balloons. The guy dove into a clump of bushes and sent the colorful orbs floating in the air. "Is there an employee basketball game or something?"

"Dude!" Flint smacked his friend's arm. "When did we get a league?"

Artie shrugged. "It must be new."

The cart slowed as the two bickered, but Doyle kept running or what he approximated as the act of running. It was more like a loping, hurrying gait. His stride changed whenever he stepped on a stone, and he now ran on the balls of his feet. Doyle tried to pay attention to the pathway's imperfections, but there were too many. He stepped on a rock that felt like the back of a stegosaurus. He yelped and hopped to a stop.

The security guards caught up and circled him in the golf cart.

"Where are your shoes?" Artie asked.

Flint leaned out from his side of the cart. "For real, dude."

"You need some flip-flops," Artie said.

The security guards weren't helping him keep a low profile. Doyle turned and scanned the area for Outfit men. "I've got to go."

Flint settled into his seat. "Dude, there's a policy about that. Bare feet are a health hazard inside the park."

Doyle pointed at the back of the cart. "Can you guys give me a lift?"

"No," Artie said. "This vehicle is for official business only."

As the cart continued to circle Doyle, families gathered to watch.

"If we gave you a ride," Flint said, "we gotta do it for everybody."

Artie motioned to the crowd. "Our cart's not big enough for all those people."

Doyle rubbed his foot against the side of his other leg. More joined to see why two security guards were hassling a guy in shorts and a T-shirt.

"Now, if you were a babe," Artie said.

Flint snapped his fingers. "Of the female persuasion."

Artie tapped one hand on the steering wheel. "That's the exception to the rule."

"You see the problem," Flint said. "We have a strict rule about dudes in our carts."

"What about a phone?"

Artie laughed. "Dude, what is with you and the rules? No personal phones."

"But you're security," Doyle said.

Flint patted his radio. "If there's a problem, we call the administration building and they call the cops. Duh."

Artie's expression turned serious, and he stopped the cart. "Do you need the police, Doyle?"

"No," he said. "What I need is to go."

"But you can't walk around without footwear," Flint said.

"My shoes are in my locker at the administration building. So you can give me a ride, or I'm gonna have to walk."

Flint turned to Artie. "That violates our no dudes in the cart rule."

Artie exhaled heavily. "What do you want to do?"

"We could go get his shoes," Flint said.

"Or lend him ours."

"No way," Flint said with a chuckle. "The dude's too big for our shoes."

"So what?" Artie asked. "He just stands here all day?"

"It's like a no-win situation, but dude got himself into this trouble. How's it our problem?"

Doyle didn't hear Artie's response. He had walked into the crowd as the two security guards continued to discuss his circumstances.

"Is that him?" a woman excitedly asked.

Doyle glanced over his shoulder.

The mother from The Terror stood off to his left. She clutched her daughter's hand, who trailed a step behind her. The rest of the field trip group was nowhere in sight.

"He's the right size," Sophia said. "That's got to be him."

"Mom, let go. You're acting crazy."

The girl tried to pull free of her mother's hand, but she held firm. Sophia squinted and leaned in as if studying Doyle's mouth. "Yango?"

Doyle shook his head, then looked away. "Wrong guy."

She straightened. "Same voice!"

"Mom, leave him alone."

Doyle searched for an escape route. There were families everywhere. Thankfully, none looked in his direction. There were also no Outfit men in the vicinity. He had to make a break for it before things got worse.

"Gotta go," he said.

Sophia's eyes widened with delight. "It's you!"

"*Mom!*" Taylor said. She yanked her hand, but her mother pulled her closer.

"It's him, honey! Trust me. We found Yango the Yeti!"

Sophia hopped up and down, but Taylor remained firmly planted to the ground.

Now, people stopped what they were doing to watch the hubbub. Sophia tossed her head about with excitement. "It's like a scene from those movies I love!"

Taylor rolled her eyes and looked at Doyle. "You should run."

Doyle stepped backward and bumped into a family that had stopped to observe Sophia's hysterics.

The mother dropped Taylor's hand and jumped toward Doyle. "Don't leave," she said and reached out for him. "Oh my! I love your tattoos."

Doyle pulled back. "Listen, lady—"

"It's Sophia," she said.

"I don't know what this is."

"You're him." Sophia excitedly pointed at Doyle's *I Survived the Terror* T-shirt.

Doyle looked down at the image of a smiling Yeti sitting at the front of a careening roller coaster.

"You're Yango," Sophia said. She briefly clasped her hands in front of her chest. "We've reconnected after I've searched for you for so long."

Taylor reached for her mom, but the woman suddenly moved.

Sophia said, "You're even more handsome out of costume." She put her hands over her heart. "I've been looking for you my whole life."

Doyle glanced around and the crowd seemed to swoon with excitement.

"Lady," he said, "we just met."

"I've searched for the essence of you since I was a little girl."

He didn't know what that meant. He stepped back, and she moved closer. He turned, but she circled with him. Every step Doyle took, Sophia countered as if they were dancing.

Several stores away, Macklin briefly appeared in a crowd. He now wore a button-down shirt with his slacks and loafers. Had the shirt been under the yellow Fun Time sweatshirt he abandoned?

When Doyle met the man yesterday, he thought his style of dress seemed odd, perhaps old-fashioned. But if he was mixed up with the Outfit, it might explain some things. From what he knew about them, they preferred to do business with square types. They would never work with the Satan's Dawgs. Perhaps Macklin himself had worked in the Outfit's orbit and had stepped out of line. That's why they wanted him so badly.

A duffel bag was slung over Macklin's shoulder as he weaved in and out of a crowd.

Doyle hurriedly moved to the right and Sophia stepped with him again.

"Don't go," she said. "I've never met anyone like you."

"We've never met."

Doyle jumped to the left and Sophia hopped with him.

"Mom!" Taylor said. "Stop!"

Macklin was getting away while Sophia acted as a defensive lineman. Doyle juked to the right, and she leaned in that direction. Doyle quickly went left, but his foot landed on a large pebble. It caught him in a tender spot, and he pulled up.

He hollered in anger. "Macklin!"

"No," she said, "My name is Sophia."

Up ahead, the big man looked over his shoulder. He slowed for a second as if to say something. Doyle raised a hand, but Macklin didn't respond. He spun and disappeared into a crowd.

"Don't run," Doyle muttered.

Sophia reached out and touched his arm. "I'm not going anywhere."

A man in a Hawaiian shirt bumped Doyle's shoulder as he sprinted by. "Outta the way, bub!"

Doyle turned just as another Outfit man bolted past. This one bumped Sophia.

"So rude!" she said.

Doyle hunched, preparing for either man to recognize him. Surely all the men in the Outfit had seen his picture now. Yet the two in colorful shirts didn't stop. They pursued Macklin into the crowd.

A golf cart skidded to a stop and Doyle turned.

Ainsley Sutherland leaped free of the little vehicle. "No running!" she hollered. She noticed Doyle, took two more steps, then stopped. "You see that?" She pointed in the direction the Outfit's men had run. "That's a safety hazard."

Sophia's arm quickly wrapped through Doyle's, and she pulled in tight to him. "We saw it all right. They bumped into us."

Doyle frowned and tugged his arm free.

Ainsley cocked her head as she studied Sophia. "Who's she?"

"I'm Yango's girlfriend." Sophia appraised Ainsley. "Who are you?"

Taylor covered her face with her hands. "Mom!"

"I'm the head of security." Ainsley glanced at Doyle. "Is this woman bothering you?"

Doyle nodded. "Yes."

Sophia's mouth opened wide. "I am not."

"Yes, Mom," Taylor said through her fingers. "You're a total stalker."

"Ma'am," Ainsley said, "I'm going to have to ask you to leave."

Sophia's face reddened. "The park?"

"The area."

"But Yango and I—"

Taylor interrupted. "That's not his name, Mom."

Sophia's lips pursed. "How do you know?"

The kid shook her head. "Yango is the Yeti."

"Maybe we have pet names for each other. You don't know everything."

Doyle rolled his eyes.

"Ma'am," Ainsley said as she crossed her arms. "You need to clear the area."

"Fine. I see whose side you're on." Sophia turned to Doyle and her head bobbled. "You don't know what you missed out on, Yango."

"I've got a pretty good idea," Doyle said.

Chagrin crossed Taylor's face as she grabbed her mother's hand. "I'm really sorry."

"Why are you sorry?" Sophia's eyes widened. "He's the one that should be sorry!"

The daughter tugged on her mother. "Let's go."

"I'm a catch!" Sophia cried over her shoulder. "A theme park actor would be lucky to get a woman like me."

Ainsley sidled up to Doyle. "Where'd you meet that one?"

"The Terror."

"Explains a lot. Opening day brings out the crazies." She looked back in the direction the Outfit's thugs had run off. "Speaking of which, who were those guys chasing?"

"Macklin."

"Who?"

"Porter."

"Why'd you call him Macklin?'

Doyle wasn't sure how much to tell her. He believed Ainsley was the type of person to get mixed up in something that could quickly spiral out of control. To protect her, he said, "I was confused," but regretted it immediately.

"Yeah," she said. "There's a lot of that going on today. So why were those conventioneers chasing Porter?"

Doyle shrugged. Now, he felt like he should say something so she wouldn't accidentally get herself into trouble if she ran across Macklin. "It's got something to do with the Outfit."

Ainsley's face darkened. "The Outfit is in Fun Time?"

"You know about the Outfit?"

"Who doesn't?" Her gaze dropped to Doyle's bare feet. "What happened to your shoes?"

"They're back in my locker."

"We have a policy against that, you know?"

"I'm aware."

She put her hands on her hips. "Why does the Outfit want Porter?"

"I don't know." That was the truth, but he still felt bad for not telling her everything he knew.

Ainsley's lips briefly pinched together. "Well, I'm going to find out."

"No, wait."

Her eyes narrowed. "Is this where you tell me to leave it alone again?" She clicked her tongue against the back of her teeth. "Look at you. Thinking I need protection. I'm the head of security, Doyle. You don't even have shoes."

"That's not it," he said.

"Save it." Ainsley hopped into her cart. "I can take care of myself." She raced away.

Doyle headed toward the administration building. He still wanted to know what was going on with Mr. Gilbert.

Chapter 10

When Doyle saw the cop, he felt a strange emotion—hope. This was especially odd after he hadn't wanted to call the police only moments before.

Prior to joining the Witness Protection Program, he felt nothing for law enforcement officers except variations of disgust and anxiety. Those feelings went all the way back to his childhood. When he was in high school, he dreaded the police.

He wasn't particularly bad then. Cops thought he was bad because he wore his hair long and his black T-shirts carried the names of heavy metal bands like Sabaton, Meshuggah, and Bloodbath. His dislike for the law wasn't totally in reaction to the way they treated him, but it certainly added to it.

When he joined the Dawgs, his dislike for police officers grew into hatred. The motorcycle club was locked in a perpetual struggle with them. The Dawgs were outlaws, and the cops were the keepers of order. Society craved safety, and the club represented everything it feared.

The Dawgs were a natural home for a kid who felt threatened by the cops. Unfortunately, his outlook changed over the years. The club rewarded profit over loyalty, and Doyle became disillusioned with his chosen family.

All of which led him to this strange moment—his spirits lifting as a police officer in a dark uniform ambled through the amusement park. Perhaps the cop had gotten a call from an attendee who saw Tony and Leo accost Yango the Yeti when they shoved him into the cordoned off area under The Summit.

Although, if an attendee had seen that kidnapping, they would likely have noticed a gun, possibly two. Panic would have run rampant through Fun Time. Yet no one seemed the least bit concerned by anything except getting on the next ride or moving closer to another funnel cake vendor. This officer strolled through the park. He wasn't in a hurry to get anywhere.

So Doyle concluded a park attendee hadn't called the police.

Maybe Ainsley had. Perhaps she called the cops after he told her the Outfit was inside the park and looking for Macklin. However, if that was true, why was the officer inside Fun Time? Had he already dealt with the thugs parked at the entrance? It was likely they simply moved on when they saw a man in uniform approaching.

Since employees weren't allowed to carry cell phones, wouldn't she have had to call the administration building to have someone contact the police? Doyle grunted. It was unlikely Ainsley was responsible.

Then why was the cop at Fun Time?

Doyle moved gingerly to intercept the officer. The balls of his feet hurt from stepping on too many pieces of gravel. Who knew such a minor thing could be such a large irritation? Who knew how much he took his shoes for granted?

Approaching a cop to talk still felt foreign. He'd done it recently—albeit reluctantly—while at his other witness protection placements. He would never have contemplated such a move while with the club.

Doyle might have developed a certain affinity for his previous witness inspectors, but he still didn't fully trust cops. They often walked into volatile situations, demanded control of it without having all the facts, and made a further mess while they found out what supposedly happened. Once the officer finally figured out what happened and unwound the additional unrest they caused, they patted themselves on the back for returning the disturbance to its original level of volatility before leaving.

This cop was in his late forties with a square jaw and salt and pepper hair. He might have been on a recruiting poster in his younger years. The man's shoulders were pulled back, and he had the easy gait of someone used to being in charge. His wrist rested on the top of his gun like a sheriff in an old western.

Many parkgoers smiled and politely waved at the officer. He motioned back in lazy ways—a dip of the chin, a flick of his fingers, or a raise of an eyebrow. The man's careless demeanor irritated Doyle because he seemed unimpressed by the public's consideration.

Doyle had never received that type of respect while a member of the Dawgs. He noticed once he cut his hair and wore less aggressive clothing that many citizens treated him differently. They smiled at him while he was in Maine, which was a pleasant change from the scowls he used to receive. He never took an act of kindness for granted the way this cop seemingly did.

He was almost to the officer when a man in a Hawaiian shirt appeared. Doyle abruptly stopped because the Outfit man eyed him. Word must have gotten out by now that Doyle had ditched the Yeti costume. Tony had sent his picture to someone who identified him as being part of the Witness Protection Program. Surely, that person had shared his photograph with everyone on the crew.

"You need something?" the goon asked Doyle. He had rounded shoulders and a single eyebrow. He tried to appear menacing, but he looked like an overworked father on vacation.

Doyle didn't appear threatening in his white *I Survived the Terror* T-shirt, blue shorts, and bare feet. There was something to be said about the leather jacket and boots he wore while in the motorcycle club. No one ever mistook him for a guy to be pushed around.

The cop crossed his arms and watched Doyle. The nametag on the officer's uniform read *Chapman*.

Doyle motioned toward the officer. "I was hoping to talk with him."

The Outfit man grunted. "Having a bad day at Fun Time, pal?" He faced the cop. "Looks like you got a customer, Chappie."

"Looks that way," the cop said.

Doyle's eyebrows rose when he heard the officer's name drop from the hoodlum's mouth.

Chapman studied Doyle. "Your kid go missing or something?"

Both the cop and the Outfit man stood shoulder-to-shoulder. It took no time for Doyle to understand the situation. "No," he said, then forced a broad grin. "Thank you for your service."

"Yeah, Chappie," the thug chuckled. "Thank you for your service."

Chapman frowned.

The Outfit's man wrapped his arm around the cop's shoulder and turned him away from Doyle. "The boss called you in, huh?"

"Geez, Vern," Chapman said. "Announce it louder, why don't you?"

"Who's gonna hear?" Vern glanced over his shoulder and glared at Doyle. "Something else, pal?"

Doyle shook his head.

"Toddle on, you." Vern waggled his fingers. "The men have things to discuss."

The two walked toward the administration building. Doyle had a bad feeling about this.

Maybe it was only some Outfit thug impersonating a cop. However, if the Outfit had its hooks into one real cop, they likely had them into more. Just how many was the question.

Was the whole Lindo Gato police department corrupt?

Doyle crouched and followed the two men.

***

Doyle passed Robbie's Ribs and Rolls when he saw the administration building. It wasn't anything particularly special to look at, especially when compared to the rest of the park. A white, single-story building with darkened windows and no landscaping doesn't pique interest when compared to the activity of Fun Time rides and games. A cluster of large palm trees surrounded the building.

He found a position behind a light pole and scanned for other men in Hawaiian shirts. He only saw families coming and going from the row of restaurants. His attention returned to the administration building.

A side door burst open, and Oskar VanLeuven stepped out. He turned back to the structure and yelled a series of expletives as the door automatically closed. Oskar pointed, kicked imaginary stones at it, then spun. He took three steps, then spun again to face the building. He swore some more while pointing and kicking again.

Several families had stopped to stare at him. One mother covered her son's eyes while the father protected the same child's ears.

Oskar raised his fist and shook it at the building. "I outta knock your teeth in, you bunch of thugs!"

Doyle snuck toward the closest palm tree. "Oskar," he whispered.

The custodial manager jumped and turned.

Doyle hid fully behind the tree. In a moment, Oskar appeared next to him. "What are you doing here?"

"Checking on Mr. Gilbert."

Oskar looked over his shoulder. "We gotta get you outta here." He grabbed Doyle's arm. "Let's go, kid. Keep your head down."

The two ran toward a smaller, rundown building behind the administration center, which wasn't easy for Doyle. Pebbles and other jagged objects poked him in the feet.

When they rounded the corner of the custodial shop, Oskar tugged an enormous set of keys from his belt. "They can't see us from here."

Oskar stole a glance at Doyle as he slipped a key into the lock. When it opened, the two stepped in. The custodial manager shut the door and flicked on the lights with a swipe of his hand.

"Look at you," Oskar said with a disapproving shake of the head. "Your work attire keeps getting worse."

Doyle grabbed the hem of his trunks. "I'm in a bit of trouble."

"But shorts?" Oskar waved a hand up and down Doyle's length. "The Outfit is riled up over this? I don't see it."

"What do you know about the Outfit?"

Oskar moved through the small building and Doyle followed him.

"I've been in Lindo Gato my whole life, kid. I know a bent guy when I see one."

"The Outfit is in Lindo Gato?"

"Who do you think built the city? Not them necessarily, but their ilk. The racketeers have been here since the early days. They wanted to make this town the Miami of the Texas coast, but that didn't work out. So they tried to make for a Vegas-light vibe, but that didn't fly, either. So, in the end, we ended up with what we are. A resort community built around a theme park."

The news about the Outfit shocked Doyle. He hadn't imagined they were in the city for so long. He'd been there for three weeks and had seen no one he would have suspected to be connected to organized crime. To be fair, he spent most of his time at the theme park or hanging out alone with his cat. Those few moments that he wasn't in those two places, he ventured to the grocery store or the used bookstore around the corner from his apartment, neither of which were likely to be hangouts for Outfit men.

If the Outfit or its ilk had built Lindo Gato, why had Krumland sent him here? Perhaps he believed there was nothing to worry about. Both Vegas and Florida had grown legitimately over time as corporations moved in and took over those cities. Or maybe Krumland was inept and didn't do enough homework on the city. Could shoddy work be the reason the marshal was on the hot seat with his superiors?

"But it ain't so bad," Oskar continued. "Having Fun Time certainly thinned out the wise guys looking for action in bigger cities."

"How do you know so much about the Outfit?"

Oskar pulled out a pair of rubber boots and threw them at Doyle's feet. "They might be too small but try them on. They're the biggest we got."

Doyle stared at him, waiting for an answer.

"My dad worked for them. I didn't like what it did to him or to my mom. That's why I did something different."

"Do the guests know what's going on?"

Oskar shook his head. "Not likely. The Outfit doesn't advertise what they're up to. That would defeat the purpose. Something big must have brought them out of the woodwork. You going to try those on our not?"

Doyle grabbed one boot.

"Why don't you tell me what you and that Macklin fella are up to?"

He paused with his foot outside the boot.

Oskar nodded. "I know his name ain't Porter. I heard the Outfit's men talking inside the administration building. So, he lied to get a job. I'd like to know what you two are doing."

"We're not up to anything. I never met the man before yesterday."

"Don't give me that." Oskar waved his hand. "Those thugs in there are sure you two are working together. They forced Gilbert to tell them I'm your boss. That's why they were giving me the third degree."

"I got wrapped into this because a couple guys thought I was Macklin."

"You two don't look anything alike."

"I was wearing the Yeti costume."

"That's right." Oskar snapped his fingers. "What happened to the dreadful thing?"

"I ditched it in one of the stores."

"For shorts and no shoes." The custodial manager chuckled. "Nice upgrade. I'd hate to watch you buy a car."

Doyle shoved his foot into the boot. His toes hit rubber before his heel could slide all the way down. He put his foot on the ground and the boot folded over.

"Not going to work, huh?" Oskar put his hands on his hips. "Let me guess. Your shoes are in your locker inside the administration building."

"Along with the rest of my clothes and the key to my apartment." Doyle kicked off the boot.

The custodial manager furrowed his brow. "You can't go in there."

"I figured. How many are inside?"

"I don't know. Eight, I guess."

Too many to fight alone, Doyle thought.

"Maybe four."

The odds swung back in his favor. He might risk it.

Oskar shrugged. "Or six."

Doyle's eyes narrowed. "Which is it?"

"I don't know." Oskar flailed his arms. "There was so much commotion and they kept moving around. Guys coming in and going out. Stick with eight to be on the safe side."

A thought occurred to Doyle. "Where'd they get the Hawaiian shirts?"

Oskar shrugged. "How would I know? And what's with those guys? Do they really think that's what people wear to the park? I'll tell you why they chose those shirts."

Doyle knew—it was to hide their guns.

"The Outfit doesn't like families and they don't like kids."

Doyle wasn't going to hold that against them.

Oskar pointed toward the administration building. "No person who has ever been to a theme park would think Hawaiian shirts and khaki shorts are common attire."

"Is Gilbert in on this?"

"Heck, no." Oskar's face pinched. "At least, I don't think so. It sure didn't look that way to me."

That wasn't the confident answer Doyle was hoping for. "What else can you tell me is going on in there?"

"They got problems. Three of their guys weren't responding. You wouldn't know anything about that, would you?"

Doyle ignored the question. "Did they say anything else about Macklin? Like why they're after him?"

Oskar smirked. "Not really. They're so frustrated they called in some of the local cops they've got on their payroll. They're making sure they catch him now that they've got him cornered."

"Is there a phone in here?"

"Yeah, why?" Oskar walked toward a work bench and moved some items out of the way. He picked up a dirty phone. He lifted the receiver from its base and pulled the tangled cord. "Calling the cops ain't going to help. I already told you they got their men on the inside."

Doyle had no interest in calling the police. "I've got some friends that can help me out of this jam."

"Some friends?" Oskar smirked. "Mr. Cryptic." He extended the receiver and base. "All right, now."

"I need some privacy."

Oskar's lip curled. "I'm not sure about you, Flanders. One minute you're a salt of the earth type. The next you're running around in an Abominable Snowman costume. Before I know it, the Outfit is after you."

Doyle held up the phone.

"Yeah, yeah. I'm going." Oskar raised a hand. "I'll be outside."

Doyle dialed a number Marshal Krumland insisted he commit to memory. It was answered on the first ring.

"Big Jake's Seafood Emporium. This is Micah. What's your customah service numbah?"

"Three forty-seven."

The U.S. Marshals created an emergency hotline service that Doyle could call whenever he was in trouble. They hid it under the guise of a business so if anyone was listening, it would sound like a normal call. Previously, the hotline had been a travel business and a psychic hotline. Doyle had recently learned other members of the Witness Protection Program had hotline cover stories different than his. Perhaps every time someone called in, the operators had to pretend to be a unique type of business. That was probably stressful on a person. Doyle never considered that before, so he thought he'd be extra kind to this operator today.

A keyboard clacked on the other end of the call. Micah inhaled sharply. "Good Lord, sir. You've ordahed a lot of our product before."

Doyle shrugged even though the man couldn't see it. "What can I say?"

"You can start with you're sorry," Micah said. It sounded as if Micah tapped his computer screen. "I mean, look it. You're obviously hogging the seafood. Maybe you didn't get any attention from your mothah so you're lashing out, but around here sharing is caring."

It's not like Doyle enjoyed calling the hotline. Doing so was admitting failure. He only called when his cover was blown. Tony the thug had sent his picture to someone who confirmed Doyle was hiding from the Satan's Dawgs. Anyone with access to the 'dirty rats' website would likely know he was currently in Lindo

Gato. He needed to leave town as quickly as possible.

Micah continued. "For some customahs, our product is so good that just one ordah lasts a lifetime, if you catch my meaning."

"It's seafood," Doyle said. "By definition, it has a short shelf life."

"Oh, that's cute." More keyboard clicking. Micah's voice sharpened. "I'm making a note of that. That was hostile."

Doyle didn't think his comment warranted that level of reaction.

"Why be that way? Was I being hostile to you?" Micah asked. "I don't think so. I was simply pointing out how much seafood you've ordahed."

"I know how much I've ordered. I don't need you to remind me."

"Nice." Micah's voice sharpened further. "Big Jake appreciates your feedback, even when it's derogatory drivel like that."

Things were quickly getting out of hand. "All right now," Doyle said, "just listen."

Micah's volume sharply rose. "Your customah service file shows previous representatives have had difficult interactions with you like I'm having now."

"What did I do?"

"Cleansing breath."

"Huh?"

Micah inhaled deeply, then counted, "One, two, three, four, five."

"You're doing that now?"

"Please don't bring your negative energy into my workplace."

"I'm on the phone," Doyle said.

"Are you minimizing my feelings?"

"Don't you guys have to go through some sort of stress training?"

Micah clucked. "Are you telling me how to do my job?"

"I'm having an emergency."

"So am I." There was more keyboard clicking.

"You're updating my file, aren't you?"

"How could you guess?" Micah asked.

Doyle furrowed his brow. "Can you get a message to Marshal Krumland?"

Micah barked a single laugh. "What is wrong with you? We're on the phone. Oh, that's totally getting added to the report."

"Okay, now," Doyle said. "Have a nice day."

"Like that's going to happen. Mister, when I file this report, you won't even know what—"

Doyle hung up.

He opened the door and Oskar looked in.

"How'd it go with your friends?"

"Wrong number," Doyle said.

"Maybe you should try again."

Doyle stepped out of the shack. "I'll call later."

Oskar watched him. "Where are you going?"

"To find Macklin so we can help Gilbert."

"But the Outfit is still after you."

Doyle didn't respond. He was already moving toward the nearest palm tree.

"Well, good luck," Oskar whispered after him.

Chapter 11

Doyle sat behind a fake palm tree on the patio of Robbie's Ribs and Rolls. He had a clear line of sight to the administration building. Four men in suits approached the structure and went inside. Things must be getting serious if more men were coming into the park and they weren't making the effort to blend in with the Hawaiian shirts and khaki shorts.

He didn't know where to look for Macklin and decided to sit still for a few minutes. Macklin could be anywhere in Fun Time. The last time he'd seen the man, Macklin was carrying a duffel. If he lugged that around, he would have a hard time going anywhere fast. He'd likely try to keep a low profile.

Were the contents of the duffel bag the reason for today's events? Was it money Macklin stole from the Outfit? If that were the case, would everything stop if Macklin gave it back? Perhaps Doyle could broker a deal and get everyone home safely. After all the commotion, though, he doubted it.

Since his picture had been run through some facial recognition software that pinged on the 'dirty rats' website, no one was going to allow Doyle to broker a deal for himself. His crime of turning against the Satan's Dawgs was too big.

"Bro!"

Doyle hunched and glanced over his shoulder.

Zeus approached in the Sassy Sasquatch costume. He pushed chairs out of his way and bumped into several customers eating lunch. Zeus didn't bother apologizing to any of them.

A gaggle of giggling children followed in Zeus's wake. Their parents stood outside the patio area and grinned with loving stupidity at their children.

Zeus spread his arms wide and bobbed the Sasquatch helmet. "You look righteous, broheim. I love the shorts. You look like you're ready to rip some waves."

Doyle slid lower in his seat. He didn't need the extra attention the Sassy Sasquatch costume brought. "What're you doing?"

The kids swarmed around Zeus and several of them jumped for his outstretched arms. None could reach them.

"Gilbert's got the whole crew looking for you, broski."

"I heard."

Zeus lowered his arms, grabbed a kid on each side, and lifted them high into the air. They squealed. "Why are you avoiding him?"

Doyle didn't want to tell him about the Outfit, so he said, "I ruined the Yango costume."

"Bogus!" Zeus lowered the kids.

"Gilbert's probably going to say the same."

"You're supposed to respect the costume, man. It's, like, the actor's code, you know?"

"I'm not an actor."

Two new kids grabbed Zeus's arms, and he lifted them into the air. These children shrieked with delight. Zeus held them off the ground for a moment. "Is that why you're watching the admin building? You want to avoid Gilbert?"

Doyle glanced back toward the squat, white building. "I'm just sitting here."

The children kicked their feet and wriggled in the air. They looked as if they weren't having as much fun as a moment ago.

"But you're not eating," Zeus said.

"It's not against the rules."

"Ha! That's funny. Porter said that, too."

Doyle furrowed his brow. "Porter said that?"

Zeus lowered the kids, and they immediately jumped for his arms again. "He's sitting in Mango Mary's."

It took a moment for Doyle to visually locate the man. Sitting at a small table on the outdoor patio of Mango Mary's Many Mixes was Macklin. He wore a blue and white Fun Time baseball hat and dark sunglasses, but it was him. He still wore that stupid plaid shirt. His attention was on the administration building.

"Gotta go," Doyle said.

But as soon as he stood and moved away from the palm tree, Macklin turned and looked at him.

Doyle moved through the patio.

Macklin abruptly stood and lifted his duffel bag over his shoulder.

Why wasn't the man running? Doyle wondered. Macklin had sprinted away earlier, but right now he seemed to wait for Doyle to get clear of the obstacles in his path. Did Macklin want Doyle to pursue him?

Doyle stepped into The Pathway of Fun and trotted toward Mango Mary's.

Macklin moved now. Not quick, but with confidence. He walked around the corner and disappeared.

Doyle picked up his pace. He stepped on something sharp and fought back a howl. He hurried as fast as he could, limping and hopping as he went. He rounded the corner but didn't see Macklin. The guy must have gone around the back of the building. Doyle ran faster now and ignored the pain in his foot.

When he turned the corner, Doyle looked left. Something heavy hit him in the back. He stumbled forward and ended up behind another restaurant. Doyle regained his footing, but before he could turn, someone kicked him in the rear. He careened forward. His arms windmilled, and he fought to keep his balance.

Something lashed out and hit his ankle. His feet tangled together, and he collapsed to the ground. Doyle skinned his knees and the palms of his hands. He rolled over and brought his fists up. The other man was just out of kicking range.

Macklin pointed at him. "Stay down."

Doyle rolled to his side and started to get up, but Macklin pulled a small gun from his pocket.

"I'll only say it once."

Doyle dropped back to the ground. This was the first time he got a long look at Macklin.

He already knew they were roughly the same size. That's why Doyle was drafted to wear the Yango costume earlier in the day. On their initial meeting, Doyle had thought Macklin looked plain. The man's hair was brown with the kind of cut provided by any cheap barber. The guy avoided eye contact and slumped his shoulders as if the world had beaten the life out of him. The few words he dared speak were soft. The only thing impressive about the guy named Porter was his size.

Now, here stood a man with a small automatic clutched in his fist. Cruelty graced Macklin's lips as if it had returned to its rightful home. His hardened glare didn't move from Doyle. His shoulders pulled back and his chest puffed out. The world couldn't beat the life out of Macklin if it tried.

"Why are they after you?" he asked.

"They think I'm working with you," Doyle said.

"Why would they think that?"

Doyle sat upright but didn't bother responding to Macklin. Instead, he checked the injuries to his knees. Blood covered his fingertips, and he wiped them across his white T-shirt.

Macklin raised the gun. "I don't have time for you to play cute."

"They fingered me as your partner when you refused to be Yango."

"I didn't put you in that costume."

"Gilbert did. That's how the Outfit decided I was your partner."

Macklin cocked his head when Doyle uttered the name of his pursuers. The gun lowered slightly. "What do you know about it?"

"I'm thinking you took something from them." Doyle lifted his chin toward the duffel bag that sat on the ground behind Macklin. "They want it back and somehow, they found you here. Did I get that right?"

Macklin shrugged.

"Now, they've locked down the park and you can't get out."

"Pretty smart for a janitor."

"Custodian." Doyle stood and Macklin took a cautious step backward. He lifted the gun again.

"Make a move," he said, "and I'll put one in your gut."

"We're in this together."

Macklin shook his head. "I'm not cutting you in."

"I don't want your money."

That seemed to confuse Macklin. He took another half-step back. "If you don't want the money, what do you want?"

So it *was* money in the bag, Doyle thought. "I want to get out of here," he said.

"I'm not stopping you." Macklin motioned with the gun. "Help yourself."

"You're forgetting something—Gilbert."

"What about him?"

Doyle thumbed over his shoulder. "They've got him in a pinch because of you."

"That's not my problem."

"But it's my problem and I'm going to make it yours until you help."

Macklin leveled the gun at Doyle's head. "The Outfit's putting the squeeze on the mayor, the chief of police, and anyone else with power in this town. You want to save them, too?"

Doyle shook his head. "Just Gilbert."

"What's so important about him?"

"He's our boss."

"Not mine."

"Have it your way," Doyle said, "but I'll be a pain in your side until you help get him free."

Macklin waggled the gun. "You might want to rethink that."

Doyle crossed his arms. "Why is the Outfit after you? Why are they dedicating so much manpower to find you?"

Macklin grunted. "There's no pleasing you, is there?" He grabbed the bag and tossed it against the side of the building. He peered around the corner before turning back to Doyle. "I guess this is as good a time as any for a break."

Chapter 12

"I'm not an actor," Macklin said. "You probably put that together by now."

Doyle's nod was barely perceptible.

"You ever hear the saying about how if things can go wrong, they will?" Macklin asked.

"Yeah."

"It feels like that's my life's motto."

Doyle smirked. The same could be said for him. Nothing had gone smoothly since he joined the Witness Protection Program.

"What do you know about the Outfit?" Macklin asked.

"They're a regional organization with their hands in a lot of cookie jars."

Macklin raised an eyebrow. "That's a lot of words to not say much."

Doyle usually didn't have a lot to say. Macklin's rebuke stung him.

"How about this?" Macklin asked. "They're like the mob but without the old-world connections. They're blinded by the value of traditions without the lessons passed through the generations. Does that sound like the group you've heard of?"

The Satan's Dawgs had a few traditions, but their history was only a couple of generations deep. Whoever sat at the head of the table could cut out any practice he deemed worthless. That happened whenever a new leader took over.

"Anyway," Macklin said, "the Outfit stretches from Florida through Texas. It occasionally battles with the mob for territory in states like Illinois, Massachusetts, and New York. The Outfit is like a cockroach. Occasionally, they get stomped on by someone bigger, but not even a nuclear war will wipe them out."

"How'd you get sideways with them?"

"Like you thought." Macklin lightly kicked the duffel bag. "I took something that wasn't mine."

"How much?"

"Enough that it hurt."

Doyle's gaze swept along the rear of the nearby buildings. There wasn't any movement back there. The steam organ music and the sounds of the amusement park rides reached them but as far as the rest of Fun Time was concerned, the two men had disappeared. Behind them was a small man-made lake. After that was the fence surrounding the park. Trees and other foliage lined the fence and made visibility difficult for passing cars.

Perhaps Doyle could swim the lake, scale the fence, and take off. But that wouldn't resolve the problem of Mr. Gilbert. He wanted to make sure the man was all right. His attention returned to Macklin.

"How'd you end up at Fun Time?" he asked.

Macklin's lips twisted. "The Outfit got their hooks into my pops. He owned a diner in Kansas City. Near the courthouse. It served cold sandwiches, soup, stuff like that. Had a great lunch crowd. If pops had kept his head down and focused on his work, he would have been fine. He and Mom would have had a good life."

Doyle shifted his stance. He hadn't expected Macklin's story to take so long. The man had barely said two words to him previously and suddenly he wanted to share his life story. The Outfit's thugs could show up at any time.

Macklin aimed the gun at something across the way and stared down the barrel. "But Pops liked betting on college football games, and the Outfit was happy to oblige with their bookies. Soon, Pops was in over his head. He couldn't pay back what he owed so the Outfit took his diner."

"All this," Doyle waved a hand toward the park, "is about a deli?"

"No, idiot." Macklin glared at him. "You think I'd go through all this for some cold cuts?"

Doyle stared at Macklin. Had the man not held a gun, Doyle might have slugged him.

"Something in those eyes tells me you're more dangerous than you let on."

"What happened to your parents?"

"I see what you did there, changing the subject."

Doyle remained silent.

"Okay, moving on." Macklin nodded. "The Outfit forced my parents to work the deli for them. Mom and Pops had to pump the cops, prosecutors, and judges who came in for a meal.

The Outfit also laundered their money through the business."

"Why didn't your parents go to the cops?"

"And be labeled rats?" Macklin smirked. "They knew the code. Our family doesn't fink."

Doyle disagreed with that sentiment. Family came before loyalty to some criminal principle. Doyle chose to work with the FBI because his grandmother was more important than the Satan's Dawgs. He didn't want to think too long about that right now.

"So what happened to them?" Doyle asked.

"They weren't any good at getting information. Pops was fidgety and Mom giggled too much."

Doyle's expression flattened. "I'm sorry."

"For what?" Macklin frowned. "Oh, no. The Outfit took the business from them and forced my parents to leave Missouri. Now, they've got nothing. They're starting over. At their age, no less."

"That's why you took something from the Outfit?"

Cruelty flared in Macklin's eyes. "I took a lot of somethings from them."

"But one of them didn't go smoothly," Doyle said.

He scratched his neck. "Most of them didn't go smoothly."

"Then why keep doing it?"

"I wanted to make them hurt."

Doyle waved him off. "What happened that led them here?"

"I hit an Outfit bank on the outskirts of Lindo Gato." Macklin studied his gun. "It was a simple operation in a strip mall. That's when I knew the hoods had their mitts into the town. The whole thing was too out in the open for the Outfit not to have someone high up in their pocket. As soon as I hit it, the cops were involved. The Outfit can't have all of them on their payroll, but they've got the chief and that's what counts. I ditched my car and ended up here."

"In Fun Time?"

Macklin nodded. "It was after hours. I scaled a fence. Found a shovel in an unlocked maintenance shed and buried my bag underneath The Summit. It had all these bushes and tall grasses around it. I thought it was perfect. I figured I'd come back for the score at another time. No one would be the wiser. Unfortunately, some of their goons caught me on the way out. We had a pretty good donnybrook before I escaped."

"And you had to come back when they started demolition on the ride."

"Less than a month later." Macklin's face pinched. "I can't tell you how many of these Outfit jobs have gone like that. It's like, if I didn't have bad luck, I wouldn't have any luck at all."

"Maybe you should stop hitting them."

"Yeah, maybe. You know, before they did what they did to my parents, I had no problem with the Outfit. I knew who they were and where they operated. I did my best to avoid them. I didn't want any trouble."

"You were a heist man before your parents lost their diner?"

"Do I look like the kind of guy who slings hash in a family café?"

He didn't. "When will enough be enough?" Doyle asked.

Macklin didn't respond. He simply stared back.

Doyle knew that look. He'd seen it plenty of times from the other members of the Satan's Dawgs. Nothing would satisfy a guy like Macklin. The same could be said of the Outfit. The two would remain locked in a struggle until someone gave up or died. Doyle believed Macklin would never willingly quit, and he knew organizations like the Outfit never died.

"I told you my story," Macklin said. "What's yours?"

"I'm just a custodian."

"Hardly. I saw what you did to that goon back there next to the carousel."

"Yango did that." Doyle shrugged. "The costume made me feel tougher than I was."

"Really? That's the story you're going with?"

"I got lucky."

Macklin studied him. "Don't want to come out and admit how tough you are? All right."

"Can we work on getting Mr. Gilbert away from the Outfit?"

"Maybe we can both get what we want—rescue Gilbert, then get out of here."

"What are you thinking?"

Macklin glanced around the corner of the building. "Well, we can't shoot our way out."

"Since we're in a theme park and there are families about."

He looked back at Doyle. "I was going to say because there are too many of them, but we'll go with what you said." Macklin glanced around the corner again. "What did you do with the Yeti costume?"

"I ditched it."

"What for?"

"Everyone was searching for it."

"Everyone?" Macklin eyed Doyle.

"You name it, and they were looking for me." Doyle waved a hand in the general direction of the park's newest ride. "With it being The Terror's opening day, the Yango costume stood out like a sore thumb."

"That's perfect." Macklin tried smiling but it seemed an unnatural act. "Where'd you leave it?"

Chapter 13

Doyle and Macklin hurried along the backs of the buildings lining The Pathway of Fun. They often leap frogged each other to make sure the way was clear for the other man. They not only worried about Outfit thugs and cops, but also Fun Time employees. Anyone in a tan and brown uniform was a potential whistleblower. When they made it to Wonder Alley, Macklin stayed hidden while Doyle returned to the Happy Hour Shop.

It was a big risk for him, but Doyle confidently stepped inside. The brass bell above the door tinkled upon his entry. He headed toward the rear of the store like it was the most natural thing for him to do.

Tabitha looked up from the counter and smiled. "It's a great day at Lone Star Family—" Her face pinched. "Nerts. It's you."

He stopped in front of her. "I left something in the storeroom."

She leaned over the counter. "You still don't have shoes. That's against the rules."

"I know."

"And you haven't paid me for the shorts and shirt—" Her eyes narrowed. "That you've got blood on." She leaned over the counter again. "Holy cow, Doyle. What happened to your knees? Did you get in a fight or something?"

"I fell down."

Tabitha looked around the store. She lowered her voice. "What kind of trouble are you in? Gilbert wants us to call in if we see you."

"It's too hard to explain."

"Well, be careful." She glanced toward the front windows. "Not everyone hates authority as much as I do."

In the storeroom, Doyle gathered up the Yeti costume. It was hard balancing everything in his hands. Before he could leave the room, the Yeti helmet and the boots fell to the floor. Doyle dropped the massive costume. He had to outsmart this problem.

He put on the wooly Yeti feet. Now, he looked like one of those high school girls who wore sheepskin boots with their shorts and T-shirts. He grunted his displeasure but there wasn't much choice. However, he had to admit his feet felt better now that they were protected. He folded the suit, stacked the helmet and paws on top, and lifted the whole mess.

Back in the store's lobby, Tabitha eyed him with amusement. "Oh, I like your outfit."

He groaned.

She pointed to a display rack. "If you're interested, we carry Fun Time lip gloss in a variety of flavors."

"No, thanks."

"Berry Berry Melon Blast is our biggest seller."

"I'll pass."

Doyle pushed open the door.

"You still owe me for the shirt and shorts!" she called.

As soon as he stepped through the door, a heavy-set man in a Hawaiian shirt bumped into him.

"Watch it, bub."

The thug's eyes dropped to the Yeti costume Doyle held. His eyes hardened and snapped to Doyle's face. Recognition set in. "Rat," he muttered.

Doyle did something against his instinct—he ran. He clutched the costume to his chest and tucked the helmet and paws underneath his chin. He sprinted along the side of the building. The heavy boots thudded with each step, and he made a heck of a racket. Doyle was lucky his pursuer wasn't a trimmer man.

"Get back here!" the hood hollered with a wheezy rasp.

"Heads up!" Doyle shouted.

"That's right. I'm gonna take your head off!"

Doyle ran around the back of the Happy Hour Shop and passed Macklin who stood with his fists raised. He spun just in time to witness the event.

The Outfit man rounded the corner like he was taking third and making a dash for home plate. He realized too late that Macklin was standing there waiting to tag him out. Macklin latched onto the thug and redirected his momentum. The hood's head collided into the back of the Happy Hour building. A strange squeak emanated from the heavy-set man before he fell to his knees and slumped over.

"He dead?" Doyle asked.

Macklin nudged him with his foot. "Not yet." He pulled out his gun.

"Whoa." Doyle scooted forward. "What're you doing?"

"He's gonna wake up in a minute and we'll have to deal with him again."

"But you don't need to do that."

"Listen," Macklin said. "You've probably never had to do this, but this is how it's done in my world."

Doyle knew exactly how it was done and he never wanted to be part of that again. Doing so now didn't fit with his journey of being a better man. "Listen, he's out cold. He's not a threat. And shooting him will be too noisy."

Macklin looked around and seemed to consider the situation. He pointed the gun at Doyle. "If he wakes up, he's your problem."

"I understand."

"You don't scare easily."

"I scare plenty," Doyle said.

"But this doesn't do it." Macklin waggled his gun. "I know there's something more to you than being a janitor."

"Custodian." Doyle tossed the costume to the ground. "Now, what are we doing with this?"

***

Doyle had heard plans like this discussed in cartoons before. He believed the guys in *Hogan's Heroes* even executed something like it once, but he might have been mistaken. He had watched cartoons and reruns with his grandmother while growing up. Regardless, there was no way this plan would work in real life. Yet, Macklin was adamant it would.

"First, we jam a stick in here."

Macklin poked a metal cane into the middle of a pushcart filled with garbage bags.

"Where'd you get the trash cart?" Doyle asked.

"Around front. Why do you care?"

Doyle didn't but it was Shiloh's. He was supposed to have dumped the bags and left the cart at the entrance to Wonder Alley. Was she still on her break? Or had she moved on to other cleaning duties?

"When did you get it?"

"While you were inside the store. May I continue?"

Doyle motioned toward the trash cart.

Macklin said, "We put the Yeti chest plate over the top of the pole like this." He hefted the upper portion of the costume over the cane.

"Where'd you get the cane?" Doyle asked.

Macklin frowned. "What's with the twenty questions?"

"I want to know."

"It's a walking stick."

"It's a cane," Doyle corrected.

"Six of one, half dozen of the other."

Doyle's voice hardened. "Where'd you get it?"

"Some old guy."

"He needs it for walking."

Macklin shrugged. "Not anymore."

"How's he going to get around?"

"What's with you? You want to get out of here or do you want to worry about everyone's feelings?" Macklin motioned to the still unconscious thug. "First, you cried over Gilbert. Now, you're upset about some old coot and his walking stick. Maybe we should go and talk about our feelings with the Outfit. Perhaps they'll let us hug our way out of trouble. Would that make you feel better?"

Doyle's eyes narrowed. "That's not what I'm saying."

"Sounds like it."

"I merely wondered if you needed to steal an old man's cane."

"Maybe I didn't. I don't know. It was there, so I took it and I'm not going to worry about it." Macklin motioned to the trash cart. "Can we finish?"

Doyle shrugged.

"Finally." Macklin put the Yeti helmet on top of the cane. It looked like half a bloody scarecrow stuck in a trash cart. "Perfect. It's the death of Yango."

It might give nightmares to some kids, but it would never fool a grown man. Doyle shook his head. It was the worst idea he'd ever heard. Up until that moment, he thought Macklin might be a smart guy. Right now, though, he was wondering if the guy had a concussion.

"It'll never work," Doyle said.

Macklin crossed his arms. "It's a diversion. It'll work. Trust me."

"The Outfit will never fall for this."

"The Outfit?" Macklin said. "No, we're not trying to get their attention. It's too hokey for them."

"Then who?"

"Have you ever been fishing?" Macklin put his hand on Doyle's shoulder. "You gotta use the right bait to catch the type of fish you want." He pointed at the trashcan Yeti. "This, my friend, is going to get Gilbert out of the administration building."

On a normal day, Doyle would have agreed with Macklin's assessment. If enough parents were upset about Yango's appearance, Gilbert would respond. "It won't work," Doyle said. "The Outfit won't let Gilbert out of their sight. They'll make him send someone else to deal with it."

Macklin tapped his temple. "You need to think like them. They're not holding him hostage, they're controlling him. They're hanging something over his head. They can let him out to deal with something like this and know he'll come back."

"So what are we going to do?"

"What you want to do." Macklin waved a hand. "We make sure he isn't one of them."

"If the Outfit is holding something over his head..." Doyle let his thought trail off.

"We'll deal with that when we get there. At least we'll know he isn't one of them. Fair enough?"

Macklin didn't wait for any further discussion of the plan. He pushed the cart around the side of the building then shoved it into the middle of The Pathway of Fun.

It didn't take long for one parent to scream.

Then another.

***

Macklin poked his head around the corner. After a moment, he pulled back and eyed Doyle. "That worked better than I thought it would."

Doyle peered around the building. Macklin was right. Standing around the trashcan Yeti were several of the custodial staff including Shiloh. She appeared distraught that her cart was in the middle of this mess.

The two security guards, Artie and Flint, were there, too. They poked at Yango and laughed while Ainsley Sutherland animatedly talked into her radio.

Mixed among the crowd of attendees were several men in Hawaiian shirts. They seemed less impressed with the scarecrow than where it might have come from. They scanned the area. Doyle prepared to pull back in case one of them looked in his direction.

"We should move," he said.

After several seconds of no response, Doyle looked over his shoulder. Macklin was gone. He was almost to the next building. The duffel bag banged against his hip as he ran.

The Outfit man on the ground stirred. "Nuh?" Before he could sit fully up, Doyle slugged him. The man crumpled back down.

Doyle sprinted now, but it was that awkward lope with the heavy Yeti boots. It was better than running barefoot, though. He wouldn't be slowed by any more jagged objects.

Both men's gaits were thrown off by additional weight. Macklin's was slung over his shoulder and Doyle's was around his ankles. Doyle would likely never have caught the other man had Macklin not paused to look around a building.

Doyle said, "Thanks for waiting—"

But Macklin didn't stick around for Doyle to finish his thought. Instead, he ran across the alleyway to the back of the next building.

Doyle grumbled to himself as he stomped after the man. He caught up to Macklin at the next building who once again waited for the coast to clear.

Macklin glanced over his shoulder. "Can you keep it down?" he whispered.

"What am I doing?"

"You're clomping like a three-legged horse." Macklin eyed the Yeti booties. "And you're breathing like an old steam engine."

Doyle balled a fist and Macklin noticed it.

"What're you gonna do with that?"

"You ought to know."

"Why don't you wait on that?" Macklin peered around the corner again. "Gilbert's coming. Take a look."

Doyle moved next to Macklin.

Louis Gilbert hurried along The Pathway of Fun. A ring of keys attached to his belt flopped with each step. Several times, he hopped around park attendees. He nodded politely and apologized as he did so, but it was clear the park manager was stressed.

"Go get him," Macklin said.

"Why me?"

"He knows you better. Stop stalling." Macklin shoved him into the alleyway.

Doyle hurried along the side of the building. When he entered The Pathway of Fun, he jostled past several families to intercept Mr. Gilbert.

The park manager stepped out of his way. "Excuse me."

Doyle grabbed his arm and spun him.

"It's you!" Gilbert looked over Doyle's shoulder toward the administration building. He lowered his voice. "You shouldn't be here. They're looking for you."

"I know." Doyle grabbed the manager by the upper arm. "Come with me."

Gilbert anxiously looked down Wonder Alley. "But there have been complaints about a Yango death mobile."

"I know. We did it to get you out of the administration building." Doyle tugged the park manager by the arm. "Follow me."

The two men hurried into the alleyway.

Gilbert pulled free of Doyle's grip. "What happened to the Yango costume?"

"It was unavoidable."

"You put it in a trash cart?" Gilbert threw his arms into the air. "It's a vintage piece!"

"Couldn't be helped." Doyle kept walking, but the park manager had stopped. "Let's go."

The manager turned back toward The Pathway of Fun. "It was one of a kind." He spun around. "Handmade in Italy. Do you know how expensive it was?"

Doyle motioned toward the back of the neighboring building. "No idea, but we had to do it."

Gilbert's eyes narrowed as he slowly walked forward. "Who's we?"

The two men rounded the corner. When the manager saw Macklin, he said, "You're still here? You said you were sick. I sent you home."

Macklin shrugged. "I lied."

"That's why they wouldn't believe me. They knew you didn't leave." Gilbert looked from Macklin to Doyle then back to Macklin. "I don't understand what's going on."

Macklin grabbed the manager by the shirt and pulled him in until the two men were nose to nose. "Are you working with them?"

"No!" Gilbert turned his face away.

"He's not," Doyle said.

Macklin shook the park manager. "Prove it."

Gilbert lifted his hands in the air. "They showed up at my office and threatened if I didn't help them find you, they'd hurt my family."

Macklin's lip curled. "I don't believe you."

"It's the truth." Gilbert closed his eyes. "I run an amusement park!"

Macklin shoved the man away. "Open your eyes."

Gilbert warily opened one eye then the second. "You're not going to hurt me?"

"Not unless you do something stupid." Macklin crossed his arms. "The Outfit's boss is in the administration building?"

"Niccolò Esposito, that's right." Gilbert looked to Doyle. "You two need to get out of here. They aim to do you both harm."

Doyle said, "We needed to make sure you were okay."

"Yeah, yeah," Macklin said and waved a hand. "Now, you got what you wanted. He's safe." He turned his attention to the park manager. "Did you overhear anything about the Outfit's plans?"

Gilbert eyed both men. "So, it's true. You two are working together."

"He's not my partner," Macklin said. "You roped him into this trouble when you put him into the costume."

Gilbert studied Doyle. "But I heard them say you were wanted."

Macklin's eyes narrowed. "Wanted for what?"

Doyle shook his head. "He misheard."

"Is that so?" Macklin turned back to the park manager. "Tell me what they said."

Gilbert's smile was nervous. "Like he said, I must have misheard."

"Tell me what they said." Macklin grabbed the manager by the shirt and pulled him in again.

"Leave him alone," Doyle said.

Macklin shook the manager. "*Now.*"

"They said he's wanted by some biker gang."

"Huh?" Macklin studied Doyle's tattoos. "A biker gang? Is that true?"

"Let him go," Doyle said.

Macklin jostled the manager without looking at him. "Explain yourself."

"I don't know. I don't know!" Gilbert closed his eyes. "They said he was a rat."

"A rat?" Macklin shoved the manager away and he lowered his head as in thought.

"It's not what you think," Doyle said.

Macklin lifted a hand. It seemed he was still trying to put together the pieces. When he latched onto something, he said, "Stay away."

"We can help each other."

"I can't get mixed up with you." Macklin lifted his bag. "I'm a thief and that's how they know me."

"Listen," Doyle said.

Macklin stepped back. "If they think I'm mixed up with an informant, then they'll label me as a snitch. I still got friends in this business. I don't need that stink sticking to me. This park is big enough for two of us. You go your way and I'll go mine. Let's not bother writing each other."

He turned and hurried into the open. Macklin didn't even worry about guys in Hawaiian shirts. It seemed he was more worried about being labeled a rat than being caught for robbing the Outfit.

Louis Gilbert said, "I'm sorry."

"It's fine." Doyle turned to find the park manager staring at the hairy Yeti feet.

"Is the costume ruined?"

"Besides the trash, I got some blood on it."

Gilbert's face flattened. "Blood?"

"It's from some of the Outfit's goons."

"I probably shouldn't have to say this—"

"I'm fired."

Gilbert put his head into his hands. "I'm probably fired, too." He looked up. "So what am I supposed to call you? Beauregard or Doyle? I heard them say what your real name was."

"Stick with Doyle. Do you have a phone I could borrow?"

"Employees aren't supposed to use personal phones in the park."

"You're the manager."

"Touché." Gilbert reached into a pocket and pulled out his cell phone. "But it's no use calling the cops. The Outfit has already called them."

"That's not who I want to call."

Doyle dialed the number he had committed to memory. It was answered on the first ring. "Big Jake's Seafood Emporium. This is Micah. What's your customah service numbah?"

"Three forty-seven."

"Ugh," Micah said, "you again."

"About that, I'd like to say—"

"Hold, please."

A dreadful song started. It was the one about the showgirl named Lola dancing the merengue at the Copacabana.

Louis Gilbert muttered, "My parents warned me about days like this."

Doyle lifted an eyebrow.

"Well, not exactly like this," Gilbert said, "but they said working at an amusement park wasn't all good times and smiles."

"What can you tell me about the Outfit?"

The park manager shook his head. "They said they were going to kill Macklin. They said you would get yours, too. That's how they said it. Just like that. 'He'll get his.' I've watched enough movies to know what they meant."

"Nobody is dying today," Doyle said.

"How can you be so sure?"

The song on the telephone abruptly stopped, and a voice came on. "Mr. Flanders?"

"Yes?"

"Hi, this is Lyle Woodbury. I'm the supervisor here at—" There was some rustling of papers on the other end of the line. "Big Jake's Seafood Emporium?" His voice was muffled now as if he covered the phone. "*Sally, is this for real?*"

"*Don't blame me,*" a woman answered from far away, "*Krumland set it up.*"

"*I wasn't blaming you. Good Lord, Krumland, what were you thinking?*" Woodbury unmuffled the phone and cleared his throat. "Anyway, I apologize for the delay in getting on the phone. I reviewed the recording of the call you had earlier with Micah."

"I understand. Listen—"

"It's important we do that, you understand. For training purposes and such."

"Right."

"And boosting employee morale."

"Hey, Woodbury," Doyle said. "I've got a situation here."

"As do we." Woodbury chuckled. "As you may know, it's hard to keep good staff. I'm not defending Micah's actions—"

Doyle lowered the phone. "Do they send you managers to any schools?"

Gilbert's face brightened. "Oh sure. Plenty." He ticked them off on his fingers. "Technology. Financial. Communicating with Millennials—"

Doyle's lip curled. He was recently called a millennial. He had been accused of a lot of things, but that was by far the worst.

The park manager continued ticking his list off on his fingers. "—Enhanced Branding through Social Media. Listening with Empathy."

Doyle lifted the phone back to his ear. Lyle Woodbury was still talking.

"—extreme turnover. So you see, I'm trying to manage customer expectations and build employee trust at the same time. It's an important skillset for a modern manager to develop—"

Doyle covered the phone's receiver and looked around. He didn't have the time to hang out here. Several of the Outfit's men were on The Pathway of Fun. It wouldn't take them long before one of them had the bright idea to check behind the buildings.

Gilbert leaned dejectedly against the building. Doyle had seen this with some of the jobs that the Satan's Dawgs had pulled when they pushed a citizen too far. A civilian could hold up only so long until they broke. Gilbert probably did fine while the Outfit had him in his office. When the call came in that there was some calamity for him to rush toward, the manager remained in his service role. However, now that things calmed, he was breaking because he had no purpose.

Doyle extended the phone. "Talk to this guy."

Gilbert frowned. "Who is it?"

"The manager of Big Jake's Seafood Emporium."

"Why did you call them?"

"Because we need their help. Just tell him who you are, that we work together, and the Outfit is here."

"But a seafood emporium?"

"Trust me. He'll make sure we get some help."

Gilbert accepted the phone and tentatively lifted it to his ear. As soon as he heard Woodbury speaking, his face brightened. "Oh, certainly. That makes perfect sense." Gilbert flashed a thumbs up. "I couldn't agree more. This Micah person sounds like a top-notch individual. I can see why you would want to retain him. Good employees are worth their weight in gold."

Doyle hurried away. The shaggy Yeti feet clomped as he did so.

Chapter 14

Men in suits stood with their arms crossed in front of two black cars. They were at the southeast entrance of the park. Doyle eyed them from his hiding spot behind a palm tree. He wasn't planning to escape. Not yet. He just wanted to get eyes on an exit and see what was there. He turned around.

The amusement park continued to thrill its attendees. Coasters zoomed up and down tracks as calliope music played. People walked with smiles and ate ice cream cones, corn dogs, and popcorn. No one seemed the wiser that the Outfit had staked out Fun Time and was hunting Macklin and Doyle.

The sun was beyond its apex now. There were only a couple of hours left before the park emptied for the night. Doyle believed the Outfit would flood the park with men then. They wouldn't have to play nice any longer because there wouldn't be any citizens with their watchful eyes and handy cell phone cameras.

Doyle didn't want to involve the law, but he had to figure out how to get Gilbert's family safe. He couldn't call the local cops, but maybe he could call the county sheriff or the state police like Ainsley had threatened. But bringing John Q. Law into the mix might bring trouble for Macklin. Doyle didn't know the man's history well enough. He'd gotten sideways with the Outfit. Was the law after him, too? Maybe Macklin and he weren't working together, but Doyle didn't want anything bad to happen to him. The Outfit guys, however, could rot behind bars.

"Was it bad?" a man asked.

Doyle shifted his gaze to him.

A little boy stood next to the man and happily ate an ice cream cone.

The father pointed to Doyle's T-shirt. "The Terror. We never made it. The line is still crazy. Kaden had some issues with a few of the mascots, so we didn't get to go on many rides today."

The boy stared at Doyle's Yeti feet.

Doyle shook his head. "I got it in one of the shops."

"Smart," the father said. "All the bragging rights. None of the lost time in line." The father started toward the exit, but the kid didn't move. "Let's go, Kaden."

"But he's—" The boy pointed at the Abominable Snowman boots.

"I know," the father said with a polite smile. "Let's not make it a big deal."

He tugged Kaden's hand and pulled him toward the exit.

Doyle hurried back into the heart of the park.

***

Ainsley Sutherland's golf cart skidded next to Doyle. "There you are." She glanced over her shoulder, then hopped off. She pushed him out of The Pathway of Fun and between two novelty stands. "Everyone's looking for you."

"I know."

"It's time you come clean and tell me what's going on."

"The Outfit is after Macklin."

She frowned. "And Macklin is Porter?"

"That's right."

"What do they want with him? And don't tell me you don't know."

"He took something from them."

"What?"

"Money."

Ainsley set her jaw. "Are you working with him?"

"No."

"Then why do they want you?"

"Because I was in the Yeti costume this morning."

She cocked her head. "Mistaken identity?"

"A couple Outfit goons grabbed me, thinking I was Macklin. Everything went downhill after that."

"Something isn't adding up."

"What do you mean?"

She jutted her hip to the side. "Who's Beauregard Smith?"

Doyle blinked twice.

"Don't play dumb," Ainsley said. "Is there someone else you guys are working with?"

"I'm not working with Macklin. And where'd you hear that other name?"

Ainsley pulled the radio from her hip and turned up the volume. A male voice said, *"Beauregard Smith, make it easy on yourself and head to the administration building."*

"They started calling for him a few minutes ago," Ainsley said.

"Maybe they're calling for one of their own."

She lifted her eyebrows. "On our radio?"

"We know you dumped the snowman costume, Smith," the voice continued. *"It's only a matter of time before we find you. Macklin, are you working with the Feds, too?"*

"The Feds?" Ainsley stared at the radio. "You think this Beauregard guy is undercover or something? Like maybe he turned informant on the Outfit?"

Doyle turned his palms upward.

Her eyes narrowed. "I'm not stupid, Doyle."

"I didn't say you were."

"You're this Beauregard person they're looking for."

"You're mistaken."

"No, I'm not. You're working undercover for the federal government."

He crossed his arms. He didn't know how to get out of this situation.

The radio crackled. *"C'mon, Macklin. We'll go easy on you if you give us back our money and turn in Smith. There's a reward for him."*

"A reward?" Ainsley cocked her head. "You must have really made them mad."

"Did you call the state police?"

She stared at him. "Don't change the subject."

"I'm not. This place is crawling with the Outfit, and it's only going to get worse after the customers leave."

Ainsley's brow furrowed. "Yeah, it's not like you can walk out with them."

"I'm stuck."

"Macklin, too." She shook her head. "I called the staties, but they didn't believe me. They thought I was a crank caller."

"Did you tell them who you were?"

"Of course, I did. When you say the Outfit has taken over an amusement park, it's not received very well. They said they'd refer it to the local police to do a safety check."

Doyle grunted. "That's great."

"What I want to know is why don't they just bring in all their men now? Most of the town knows the Outfit operates here."

Doyle knew why. "Because everyone has a phone, and the Outfit can't put all those people under their thumb. A parkgoer might take a picture or a video of one goon doing something stupid and post it on social media. Then word would get out that something bad went down at Fun Time. The Outfit needs to operate in the shadows. If they're exposed, the truth comes out and the pressure will come from the Justice Department."

"Social media doesn't have that much power." Ainsley smirked. "You've been watching too much TV."

But he knew the truth. Social media had ruined several of Doyle's previous identities. He imagined the Outfit felt the same way. They would want to catch Macklin and recover their money. They'd also want to grab Doyle for the favors they'd garner with the mob. But they wouldn't risk doing either at the expense the publicity would bring. That's why they had dressed most of their men in the silly Hawaiian shirts and khaki shorts and had taken their time in finding Macklin and Doyle.

An idea came to him. "I need a phone."

"Why?"

"To call a friend."

Ainsley cocked her head.

"A friend in law enforcement." Doyle had never said more confusing words in his life.

**

Doyle sat on an upside-down bucket. Opened bags of Doritos and Oreos were spread about on a turned-over cardboard box. The small building was big enough for only two people to sit comfortably. It was on the backside of Sassy Sasquatch's Tower Drop of Doom. It smelled musty. A thin layer of dust covered most of everything.

"What is this place?" Doyle asked.

"It's a maintenance building," Ainsley said. "There are several of them around the property."

Doyle smirked. "Maintenance guys. You sure they're real?"

"Of course, I'm sure. Look around." She motioned to the opened bags of snacks.

"I've been here for weeks, but I've never seen them. I see us custodians doing our jobs, and you security types—"

"Naturally."

"And the mascots."

Ainsley rolled her eyes. "Ugh."

"The store vendors, too. But we never see the maintenance guys."

"What can I tell you?" She shrugged. "They're always fixing something. If you saw one of them standing around, it would probably mean something was in danger of breaking."

Doyle grunted. "I don't know."

"You're overthinking it." Ainsley pointed to a green phone hanging on the wall. Its long spiral cord was a tangled mess. "Make your call."

He walked over and lifted the receiver. Next to the phone was a small panel with a label that read *Park Broadcast System*. It contained a microphone, a speaker, and a volume dial.

Doyle stared at the phone's illuminated keypad. He wasn't sure of the number any longer. He had memorized it months ago but had never found a reason to dial it. The last digit didn't feel right—was it a seven or a nine? He decided it was a nine.

Doyle tapped in the numbers. The call was answered on the third ring.

"Szechuan Palace," a woman with a thick accent said. "How can we take your order today?"

Doyle hung up and redialed. This time he used a seven as the last digit. This call was answered on the first ring.

"What?" a man said gruffly.

"Hello?" Doyle asked.

"Wrong number." The phone went dead.

Doyle hung up. Maybe the last digit was a four.

"This is your plan?" Ainsley asked. "Keep dialing random numbers until someone answers?"

"I got it." Doyle dialed again.

The phone rang until it went to voice mail. There was no friendly greeting, just a computer-generated voice that said, *At the tone, leave a message.* No name was provided before a long beep.

"Hi, it's—" Doyle glanced at Ainsley. "Well, you know who it is."

She slapped her hands together. "I knew it! You're that Beauregard fella."

He continued. "When you get a chance, call me at—" Doyle read the handwritten number on the base of the phone. "It's important. Life and death important." He hung up the receiver.

Doyle stared at the phone, hoping it would immediately ring back.

"So what is it?" Ainsley asked. "Wait. Don't tell me. Let me guess." She pointed at him. "You're on the run from an ex-wife and avoiding child support payments."

"What?"

"No. That doesn't make sense." She shook her head. "It's gotta involve the Outfit, right?" Ainsley held up her hands. "Let me think." She snapped her fingers as she thought. "You robbed a bank."

"No."

Ainsley frowned. "You sure you didn't rob a bank?"

"I'm sure."

Her lips twisted as she studied Doyle. "You look like you could have."

Now he glared at her.

"But you're Beauregard Smith."

"I never said that."

"You didn't have to. I figured it out on my own."

Doyle set his hand on the phone, willing it to ring.

Ainsley leaned in to get his attention. "Are you going to tell me what you did?"

"I didn't do anything."

"Then why do you have a fake name?"

Doyle frowned. "It's not fake."

"You have two names? How's that possible?"

The phone rang, and Doyle answered it. "Hello?"

"Long time, no speak," Special Agent Maxwell Ekleberry said.

"Tell me about it."

Ekleberry was the man who started everything. He had found Doyle's weakness—his grandmother—and used it to turn him against the Satan's Dawgs. At the time, Doyle hated Ekleberry. There might have been no one he despised more in the world. However, the longer he'd been away from the club, the more Doyle realized the lawman might have saved his life—in more ways than one.

"Last I heard," Ekleberry said, "a marshal pulled you out of Belfry, Oregon. I lost track of you after that. How you doing?"

"Not so good."

"What's going on?"

Doyle eyed Ainsley. "I'm at Lone Star Family Fun Time."

"That's a mouthful. I'm guessing it's an amusement park in Texas."

"That's right."

Ekleberry chuckled. "Who'd you tick off to get placed there?"

"The new guy."

"The way you're talking makes me believe someone is there with you."

Ainsley watched Doyle suspiciously.

"That's right," he said.

"Got some trouble brewing?" Ekleberry asked.

"The Outfit is here."

"That's interesting. Whoever is there with you knows about the Outfit, but they don't know you're in the program?"

"That's right," Doyle said. He smiled at Ainsley.

She eyed him with skepticism.

"Do they know you're talking to the FBI?"

"No."

Ekleberry laughed. "The trouble you get in, Beau. So, where is this amusement park?"

"Lindo Gato."

"Are you kidding? I don't get the names of Spanish towns. What the heck does that even mean? Something cat?"

Doyle didn't know. He thought *gato* was Spanish for gate.

"And why does the Outfit even care about you?" Ekleberry asked. Before Doyle could answer, Ekleberry said, "Wait. They found you on the 'dirty rats' website."

"That's right."

"How the heck did they do that?"

"They mistook me for some guy named Macklin—a heist man who's made it a mission to go after them."

"Hold on, I'm writing all this down."

For several moments, Ekleberry was quiet on the phone. Ainsley tapped her foot as she watched Doyle. He smiled again at her, but that only reinforced her suspicions.

"All right," the FBI man said. "Anything else?"

"The Outfit is threatening to harm the park manager's family unless he works with them. Can you get someone to check on them to make sure they're okay? His name is Louis Gilbert."

"Uh-huh. Got it. If you're calling me about all this, I'm assuming the Outfit has the exits blocked and, for some reason, you can't call the local cops."

"The Outfit has their hooks into them. We don't know who we can trust."

"Why didn't you call your witness inspector?" Ekleberry asked. "Don't they have a hotline for this?"

"There was a breakdown on the line."

"Technology." The agent snickered. "That's why you called me. There's no way I can get to you fast enough. I'm not anywhere close, but I'll make some calls. Maybe see if someone out of the Austin or San Antonio offices can help."

Doyle lifted his head. He wasn't particularly excited to talk with another FBI agent, but any help to eradicate the Outfit would be welcomed. "I'd appreciate it."

"If you saw this going down some way," Ekleberry said, "how would you see it playing out?"

"Loud, with lots of news coverage."

Ekleberry was silent for a moment.

The park's speaker crackled. "*Welcome to Family Fun Time, the Lone Star State's—*"

Ainsley flicked the volume dial and cut off the broadcast.

"Okay," Ekleberry said, "I think I get what you're suggesting. Is this a good number to call you back at?"

"Right now, it's the only one we've got. If I'm not here, talk with the woman who answers.

Ainsley's mouth dropped open.

"Her name is Ainsley," Doyle said. "She's the head of park security."

"Making new friends," Ekleberry said.

"It's not like that."

"I was going to say, whatever happened to that woman from Pleasant Valley?"

"I'd like to know."

"I hear you," Ekleberry said.

"I'm serious," Doyle said. "I'd like to know."

Ekleberry grew serious. "Beau, sometimes the heart doesn't get what it wants, you know that. One of you stay by the phone." The lawman hung up.

Doyle set the receiver back in place.

Ainsley moved closer. "What kind of friend was that?"

"That was Special Agent Max Ekleberry."

"The FBI? You *are* that Beauregard guy!" She pointed at him. "Wait. Are you some sort of super cop?"

"He's going to call back with information. I need you to stay here until he does."

Her brow furrowed. "Why am I waiting here?" She pointed at the door. "I'm the head of security. Fun Time is my responsibility. I need to be out there."

"You can't help with what I'm going to do."

"Which is what?"

"I'm going to take the fight to the Outfit until help arrives."

Ainsley's face pinched with concern. "How are you going to do that?"

"I don't know yet. I'll make it up as I go along."

"But why do you need to do that?" She waved her hand about. "They don't know about this place. You can stay here until help arrives."

"Hiding isn't my style."

"Staying by the phone isn't mine either."

Doyle inhaled deeply. "Please."

Ainsley crossed her arms. "Fine, but I'm only doing it because you're a federal agent and outrank me."

He kept his expression flat. Now wasn't the time to correct her.

"What do I do after he calls?" she asked. "You don't have a radio." Ainsley glanced around the little shack. "And there are no spares here."

"Come find me."

"How will I do that?"

"Follow the commotion."

Doyle opened the door and poked his head out. No one was in sight.

"Doyle," she said.

He looked over his shoulder.

"You probably don't need me to say this—"

Doyle held up hand. "I'll do my best to stay safe."

"Well, yes," she said, "but... don't take my golf cart."

"Right."

He stepped outside and pulled the door closed behind him. He headed for The Pathway of Fun. Sounds of the amusement park overwhelmed him—clacking roller coasters, cries of joy, and the annoyingly hopeful sounds of the steam organ.

Chapter 15

Blending in is an art.

When Doyle first joined the Witness Protection Program, he looked like an outlaw with his sleeve of tattoos on full display. Over his black-on-black ensemble, he vainly sported the club's cut—a leather vest which carried a large patch with an image of a horned dog baring its teeth. It was the Satan's Dawg's uniform, and he wore it with pride.

Before he arrived in Pleasant Valley, Maine, Marshal Onderdonk prepared Doyle for his life in witness protection. He insisted Doyle cut his hair and shave his beard. He also suggested he wear long-sleeved, button-up shirts to hide his tattoos along with khaki pants to look like a regular citizen. In other words, the lawman wanted Doyle to dress as a nerd to fit in with the locals. Yet he never completely blended in with that Northeastern crowd. His size and demeanor made him stand out in a town mostly populated with elderly folks.

Doyle blended in well with the Fun Time's custodial crew. Most of them had tattoos, and no one cared he was tall. Also, none cared he had a proclivity to wear black T-shirts or jeans on his personal time. When he came to work, he put on the park's tan and brown uniform and melded into the background. Fun Time attendees never noticed the custodians. People failed to see those who cleaned their offices or their hotel rooms. It made Doyle's life easy.

Now he had a hard time blending in with the park's guests. A couple of men were taller than him, but they looked like traditional dads—oversized shirts, khaki shorts, and running shoes.

Doyle looked like a demented gym teacher in his white T-shirt with its bloody smears, blue athletic shorts, and hairy Yeti boots.

The husbands eyed him with distrust and pulled their wives closer. There were several single mothers who seemed oddly fascinated by Doyle's appearance, but their children tugged them toward the rides and games.

If blending in was an art, Doyle was a fingerpainter at best.

He approached the plywood fence surrounding The Summit. The lock hung open in the hasp, and the gate sat slightly askew. Doyle glanced left and right, checking for Outfit men. Not seeing any, he moved toward the opening. He heard voices inside. It was hard to make them out due to all the noises in the park, but Doyle tried.

"What took you so long?" a deep voice said. It was Leo.

"Yeah," a smooth voice added that clearly belonged to Tony. "We were in here forever."

Doyle quietly removed the lock from the hasp. He would push the gate closed, slip in the lock, and trap the men in there again. It wasn't a major diversion, but even small ones like this could cause issues for the Outfit. It would take men time and energy to open it again.

A new voice spoke now, and Doyle leaned closer to hear better. Some kids screamed as a roller coaster zoomed down some nearby tracks.

"You weren't in here forever," the unfamiliar voice said. It was raspy, like a car driving over gravel. "That's hyperbole, Tony."

"Okay, whatever, Lincoln. We were in here a long time. Is that better?"

"We had to track down the janitor so we could get some keys. You should be grateful we went out of our way for you."

Doyle was about to close the gate and lock the goons inside when he heard a voice he knew.

"You got what you wanted," Oskar VanLeuven said. "Can I go now?"

Lincoln laughed. "Your park has a rat problem, Mr. Janitor."

A burst of music forced Doyle even closer to the fence. He dared a look inside The Summit. Three goons surrounded Oskar.

Leo and Tony seemed worse for wear. Blood smeared their faces. Their hands were empty, so they hadn't recovered the guns that Doyle had thrown under The Summit.

Lincoln was a short, thick-waisted guy in a gray suit. He might have a gun under his jacket, but his hands were currently empty. He gestured as he spoke.

"I don't know what you're talking about," Oskar said.

"A thieving rat and a dirty rat," Lincoln said. "And you're going to help us exterminate them."

Oskar didn't seem like much of a fighter, which meant Doyle had to get involved if the man hoped to get free. Three against one. Doyle didn't like the odds, but he'd fought worse.

He hefted the weight of the stainless-steel lock.

Doyle's plan was simple. He'd step inside the gated area and bean Lincoln in the head with the lock. If it immobilized the man, Doyle would consider it fortunate. If it did not, the man would likely be temporarily distracted. He would deal with Tony and Leo then. Both men still appeared woozy from their earlier beatings. They shouldn't put up much of a fight.

It was a good plan, and Doyle was confident it would work.

Doyle stepped around the gate and reared back with the lock. Oskar saw him enter and his eyes widened. The three thugs spun to face him.

"It's him!" Leo hollered and pointed at the Abominable Snowman feet.

"Bumble!" Tony said.

Lincoln's eyes narrowed. "The rat."

Doyle threw the lock with the confidence of a major league pitcher. It sailed over Lincoln's head and under the partially dismantled Summit.

Oskar covered his head and ducked.

"What the—?" Lincoln shouted. He didn't get to finish the sentence because Doyle lunged at him.

"Arrgh!" The Yeti cry was unnecessary as Doyle only wore the boots, but something in the moment resonated with him.

Lincoln didn't try to defend himself. Instead, he reached for his waistband.

Doyle immediately threw a four-punch combo—a jab, cross, hook, and uppercut. Lincoln stiffened and fell backward. He hit the ground with a heavy thud.

Tony and Leo had stayed rooted in place during Doyle's initial attack. However, when he faced them, Tony bolted toward the gate.

Leo didn't move, however. He shook like a scolded chihuahua.

Doyle took two enormous steps and jumped for Tony. Again, he growled, "Arrgh!" This was partially for Leo's benefit and because Doyle was getting into the moment. His hand hooked the back of Tony's Hawaiian shirt and yanked the man downward.

Tony slammed to the ground but didn't lose consciousness. The man lifted his hands to protect his face. "You'll regret this, Bumble!"

Doyle punched him and Tony passed out as playful steam organ music drifted over the plywood walls.

Leo stood in place. He raised his arms in surrender.

"You okay?" Doyle asked Oskar.

The custodial manager nodded. "A little shook up."

"We're getting out of here." Doyle bent and searched Lincoln's pockets. He found the man's cell phone. He didn't have a pocket to tuck it into, so he tossed it to Oskar. "Here."

The manager immediately dropped it to the ground and stomped on it.

Doyle stared at him.

"Didn't you want me to do that?"

"No."

Oskar stared at the broken phone bits that surrounded his foot. "I didn't think you'd want them calling us on it and tracking us in the park." He shrugged. "They do that in those shows."

Doyle pulled the gun from Lincoln's waistband and stood. He wasn't going to hand this to Oskar. Who knew what the man might do with it? Earlier in the day, he had thrown away Leo and Tony's guns. He was going to keep this one for now.

He turned and studied Leo. Doyle noticed earlier that the man stood roughly the same size as him. His Hawaiian shirt was kitschy orange and white, and his khaki shorts fell below his knees. His loafers were scuffed, and his socks slouched below his ankles. Doyle pointed the gun at Leo. "Gimme your shirt."

Leo reached for the first button. "All right, bub. Take it easy."

"Your shorts and shoes, too."

"My shoes? Ah, c'mon. These are Santonis imported from Italy. They're my favorite pair." Leo pleaded.

Doyle cringed at the description of the double-buckle loafers. If he was still in the

Dawgs, he might have smacked the guy up just for wearing them. But Doyle looked down at his Yeti feet, then at Leo's. He cringed when he muttered, "The shoes."

This was one of Doyle's lowest moments since joining the program.

**

Doyle pushed the gate closed and slipped the lock into the hasp. Leo and the other thugs were still inside. Oskar had run off to check on his staff.

"Oh," a woman said, "I like your outfit."

Doyle spun and found himself face-to-face with Sophia and her daughter.

A smile spread across her lips, and she blinked several times. "You're more handsome than *Magnum P.I.*"

"Mom!" Taylor said.

She waved off her daughter. "Well, he is." Sophia cocked her head. "It must be kismet how we keep running into each other."

Taylor rolled her eyes and looked away. "Don't be so weird, Mom."

Doyle locked the gate to The Summit. "I've got to go."

"Where are you off to in such a hurry?" Sophia asked.

Taylor looked at the sky. "What's it matter, Mom? He's busy."

Sophia eyed her daughter. "A man dressed like that isn't busy." She waved her hand up and down Doyle's length. "The shirt and shorts say he's ready for relaxation, but I will admit the socks and loafers give off some confusing signals."

Doyle thumbed in the general direction of the administration building. "Listen, lady, I've got to go."

"Lady?" Her brow furrowed. "You don't remember my name?"

Doyle glanced at Taylor. Even the daughter seemed stunned by her mother's question.

Sophia jutted her hip to the side and stuck her hand on it. "Now, you listen to me, Yango. I've given you the better part of my day, traipsing all over this park, back and forth, looking for you." Her head bounced about as she spoke. "And this is how you repay me?"

Doyle thought about saying he was sorry, but he didn't want to encourage the conversation any further. Besides, several attendees had stopped what they were doing to watch Sophia. He scanned the crowd for Outfit men.

"Is there somebody else?" Sophia asked.

"Now that you mention it—" A harmless lie about Daphne Winterbourne right now wouldn't hurt.

Sophia's face tightened. "It's that security guard."

"Mom!" Taylor took several steps away and stopped.

Doyle headed in the opposite direction, but Sophia followed.

The crowd parted for him as Sophia hurried alongside.

"Well," she asked. "What's her name?"

"Leave him alone," Taylor hollered from behind them.

Doyle cast a sideways glance. "We don't even know each other."

"Then why are you worried about her?" Sophia asked.

"I'm talking about me and you."

She pulled back aghast but didn't slow walking. "We know each other. Besides, how can we get to know each other better with her in the middle of everything?"

"Mom!" Taylor called. "People are watching!"

More guests stopped to observe the scene the woman was making. Doyle cringed. This was the opposite of keeping a low profile.

He struggled to keep his voice calm. "If you must know, there's a woman I like."

"You like?" Sophia pshawed. "That's all? There are literally dozens of guys I like. Big deal." She tapped her thumb against the inside of her third finger. "Until there's a ring on it, we're on the market."

"That's not how it works."

"Yes, it does."

"Not for me."

The words weren't a lie. He'd not always been this way, though. The old Doyle usually had more than one woman. That was the way of the Dawgs. But Doyle didn't want to be that man any longer.

Sophia appraised him the way a farmer might judge a steer. "It's clear you need a woman. Earlier, you were running around with no shoes and now you're dressed like a reject from an insurance convention cookout." She inhaled sharply and covered her mouth. "But you're pulling it off in the most delightful way."

Doyle glanced around. Now that they were talking in a softer tone, the other attendees seemed less interested in them. "You're barking up the wrong tree."

"Is that so? You think she's Mrs. Right?"

"I don't know." Thoughts of Daphne Winterbourne drifted through his mind. "Maybe. Yeah."

Sophia smiled. "Ah, that's sweet. I'll tell you what." She lowered her chin and her eyes darkened. "Until you work it out with her, I'll be Mrs. Right Now. How about that?"

Taylor grimaced. "Ew. Gross."

Doyle waved once. "Gotta go." He turned again.

"Hear me out," Sophia said.

He needed to get rid of this woman and her kid, but he wasn't going to out run her. He stopped. "Lady—"

"It's Sophia. I thought we established this?"

"—you seem nice."

"Thank you for noticing." She smiled.

"But this will never work." He waggled his finger between her and him.

"Why not? You just said I was nice."

Doyle didn't want to be rude. Part of being a better man was trying to avoid hurting people's feelings. So he pulled out a proven answer from a previous placement. "Store policy."

Her brow furrowed. "What?"

He waved a dismissive hand. "Park policy."

"I don't understand."

Taylor approached her mother's side now. Sophia absently reached out for her daughter and pulled her closer. Worry crossed the mother's face as if she expected bad news.

"Yeah," Doyle said, "the park doesn't allow its employees to—" He searched for a word to communicate the idea of mingling without saying it to provoke an unwanted reaction. "Well, you know."

"Fraternize?" Sophia said.

"That's it," he said. "The park doesn't allow its employees to fraternize with the guests."

"That's the stupidest rule I've ever heard," Sophia said.

It was stupid, Doyle agreed, but he nodded anyway. "Park policy," he said. "What are you going to do?"

"I'll tell you what I'm going to do."

Taylor's eyes widened. "Oh, no."

Doyle's gaze snapped to the kid.

Sophia pointed at Doyle. "I'm going to protest that policy."

He scrunched his nose. "That's not a good idea."

"Oh, it's a good idea." Sophia nodded.

Taylor shook her head. "No, it's not."

The mother repeatedly jabbed the air with her finger. "You don't know who I am. I fought with the school board when they tried to change the policy about the drop-off times. Who won?"

"You?" Doyle guessed.

"You bet I did. And who won when I fought the grocery store about their policy of returning a half-eaten sausage?"

Doyle glanced at Taylor, who nodded sadly.

"So," Sophia continued. "I'm gonna walk into that office and give the park manager a piece of my mind. I'll get that policy changed."

"You shouldn't," Doyle said.

"I will," Sophia said. "I most certainly will. For us. For my daughter."

"Don't drag me into this," Taylor said.

Doyle motioned toward the kid. "Listen to her."

Sophia pulled Taylor closer. The girl looked like a hostage. "Which way to the office?"

Doyle didn't want to send the two of them there while the Outfit was using it as their Fun Time headquarters. Who knew what they would do if they discovered Sophia had a make-believe connection to him? He said, "It won't do you any good to go to the office. The park manager isn't there."

"Where is he?"

Doyle briefly thought about it. "The Terror."

Suspicion clouded Sophia's eyes. "How do you know?"

"I was just there," he lied.

Taylor looked up at her mother. "Maybe I can ride it this time?"

Sophia's shoulders slumped. "Ugh."

"That's why we came."

"But that line," the mother said.

"We ditched the group to find him." Taylor waved at Doyle.

"Fine." Sophia inhaled deeply. "You stand in line while I deal with the manager."

Taylor shrugged. "Like that's a punishment."

Doyle backpedaled.

Sophia reached for him, but he was too far away. "We're not done with this discussion, Yango!"

"That's what I'm afraid of," Doyle muttered.

The mother and daughter headed toward Fun Time's newest ride. Doyle turned and ran in the opposite direction.

Chapter 16

The Hawaiian shirt and khaki shorts were a horrible combo by themselves, but the black socks and scuffed loafers made Doyle feel like an accountant on an island excursion. An occasional park guest cast a judgmental glance his way. A mid-thirties man walking alone through Lone Star Family Fun Time was strange enough. Adding this clothing to the mix gave others something to be worried about.

Doyle headed toward the administration building. The gun tucked into the back of his shorts felt oddly comforting, like the voice of an old friend. In his quest to be a better man, Doyle disliked moments that reminded him of his past. When he was the bookkeeper for the Satan's Dawgs, he always carried a weapon. Reasons for that were twofold: he never knew when people might wish to do him harm, and he never knew when he might be asked to clear the books on someone.

Now that he wanted to be a different person, he didn't need to carry a weapon. Here in Fun Time he was being forced to do so.

Doyle knew that was a lie. He wasn't being forced to do anything. Only earlier he had thought it reckless for the Outfit's thugs to bring guns into the theme park. Yet he didn't want to dismantle the gun in front of a still conscious

Leo. That would have only encouraged him to put it back together. No, Doyle took this one. Underneath his desire to be better remained a man of action.

What was his plan exactly? To create mayhem until help arrived. Mr. Gilbert was out of the administration building, but that didn't ensure the manager's family was safe. Macklin could take care of himself. Once aid arrived, Doyle would head home, grab his cat, and leave Lindo Gato for good.

Overhead, the speakers crackled. *"Is this thing on?"* a man asked. *"Right."* He cleared his throat. When he spoke, he sounded older, but his words carried authority. *"Beauregard Smith, report to the administration building toot sweet."*

Doyle stiffened and glanced around.

The park goers paid no attention to the announcement. They continued on their ways.

His gaze drifted up to the speakers, but there was no further information.

"They're calling for you," a man said.

Louis Gilbert approached. He looked around, then leaned in. "If they ask, I'll say I never saw you."

"How'd you find me?"

Gilbert pointed. "You left me behind that building over there. Remember?" When he faced Doyle again, he pulled back. His gaze traveled Doyle's length. "On your way to a luau?"

"It's a disguise."

"You're trying to blend in as what—an old sofa?"

Doyle frowned. "What did Lyle Woodbury have to say?"

"Boy, that Seafood Emporium manager is such a wonderful individual. I'm not sure how much business you do with them—it sounds like you're a repeat customer—but they said they were rushing an order to you."

A weight lifted from Doyle's shoulders. "They give an idea of how long it would be?"

"Several hours at least. They said they'd hurry someone out from Austin."

"They don't have anyone closer?"

Gilbert shrugged. "It surprised me they had a Seafood Emporium there. That's sort of far inland for an emporium, don't you think? Shouldn't there be one in Galveston, right on the gulf? Wouldn't that make the most sense?"

Doyle didn't know his way around Texas yet and hadn't familiarized himself with a map of the state either.

"Anyway," Gilbert said, "Mr. Woodbury suggested you relax; they'll have you taken care of in a jiffy."

"The park will close in less than three hours."

"Yeah. So?"

Doyle didn't feel like explaining his fears to the park manager. If he wanted to stay alive, Doyle needed to take the fight to the Outfit now. "I've got to go."

"Where are you going?" Gilbert asked. "Hey, I'm not sure what you're going to do with an order of seafood, but I can't wait to see."

"I'm headed toward the administration building."

Gilbert's eyes narrowed. "The Outfit is there."

"I need to keep them busy, or they're gonna keep looking for me."

"That doesn't make any sense."

"Trust me."

The park manager shrugged. "Okay. Is there anything I can do to help?"

"Stay away from me and Macklin."

Gilbert dismissively waved a hand. "Don't worry about me."

"I'm worried about your family."

"Right." The manager seemed to have forgotten about them. "Yeah, I probably shouldn't rock the boat, huh?"

"Don't give the Outfit any reason to hold a grudge against you. Your best bet is to manage the park."

Gilbert smirked. "That's not very glamourous, now is it?"

"It's important," Doyle said. "There are a lot of people here today. They came because Fun Time promised them an experience with The Terror."

"It's all gone wrong because of the Outfit."

"That's how it always goes with those types," Doyle said. "Do you want these families to have the best day of their lives, or will you let the Outfit take it away from them?"

Gilbert nodded. "I thought I had planned for just about every contingency."

"It's tough to plan for the Outfit." Doyle patted the manager's shoulder. "Take care of yourself."

***

Things can always get worse. That was a truism a fellow prisoner once told Doyle,

Armon Grimly wasn't a kind man. It's difficult to find gentlemen behind bars, and Grimly had lived most of his adult life in state prison. He earned the nonthreatening nickname 'Bruise' for the way his skin purpled and blackened whenever he bumped into a table or cot. This garnered him an unfair amount of attention whenever new inmates discovered the origin of his moniker. Most fish were eager to establish a reputation upon entering a new facility.

That alone might define the truism Bruise shared one afternoon. However, Bruise never related philosophies to stories of himself. He always used another man as an example to make his point.

A new inmate approached Bruise one afternoon and punched him while he sat at the lunch table. Doyle also was new to the facility but never established his reputation that way. He figured enough men would come in search of him for his size. Eventually, he would fight, and the rest of the prison would know not to mess with him any further.

Bruise rolled with the punch and collapsed onto the table. His tormentor danced with his hands in the air. The new inmate wasn't paying attention when Bruise unexpectedly rose from the table and stabbed him in the eye with a fork. While the injured inmate writhed on the floor in excruciating pain, Bruise returned to the table.

He picked up a piece of buttered cornbread and studied Doyle. With a nod to the injured man, Armon 'Bruise' Grimly said, "Things can always get worse."

That truism returned to Doyle as a phalanx of Lindo Gato police officers strolled through the amusement park. Several of the cops carried two photographs. One officer stopped a tall guest, then motioned for another cop to come closer. The two compared the pictures to the tall man's face, then pushed him away.

The accosted guest asked a question that Doyle couldn't hear. The cop flicked his hand at the citizen and walked away.

It wasn't hard to guess who was on the photographs.

Doyle stepped into the closest store and backed in. He didn't want to take his eyes off the cops in case one of them noticed him.

"Welcome to Fun Time, sir," a woman said. "Is there anything I can help you find?"

He looked over his shoulder at Tabitha, the young woman with jet black hair.

"Nerts. It's you." She rolled her eyes. "What are you going to steal this time?"

He glanced about the store—it didn't seem anyone else was there with them. Doyle returned his attention to the window, but Tabitha's words lingered in his ears. "I still owe you for the shirt and shorts," he said. "I didn't forget."

"I see you got some different threads. Lose a bet or something?"

Doyle glanced down at his colorful shirt.

"I think Hawaii should sue the manufacturer for false representation of island life."

Overhead, the speaker crackled. When the park made announcements, it cut into the stores as well. A male voice said, "*Beauregard Smith, report immediately to the administration building. We found your girlfriend and daughter.*"

Doyle straightened.

"Boy," Tabitha said, "that Beauregard guy is in trouble. The guy lost his girlfriend and daughter. That will not play well at the dinner table. Imagine the earful she's going to give him tonight."

Girlfriend and daughter? Doyle squinted, thinking. Then he realized who they meant.

Sophia.

"It's like my mom and dad," Tabitha said. "Whenever he lost us, my mom would nag him like a chicken on a June bug. To be fair, half the time Mom was trying to ditch Dad whenever we went, so he probably thought we'd abandoned him. Our family is complicated."

His attention returned to the window. Several cops were nearing the store.

Doyle backpedaled. "Mind if I use the storeroom again?"

Tabitha cocked her head. "What have you got going on back there?"

He hurried past the shelving units and opened the storeroom door. He jumped when he saw the dirty, bloody Yeti costume draped over a stack of boxes. The dead eyes of the helmet stared at him. Doyle frowned. He hadn't left it there. The last he saw of the Yango costume, it was sitting in a garbage cart acting as a scarecrow. Doyle felt stupid for being surprised by the costume. Thankfully, no one had seen his reaction.

Doyle didn't close the storeroom door completely. He left it open slightly so he could hear if the cops entered.

His thoughts returned to Sophia. Would it be bad if he escaped and left her in the clutches of the Outfit? It wasn't exactly what a better man would do, but Doyle thought he could get over any feelings of guilt or remorse as strange as they sounded.

However, if what the Outfit said was true, they had Sophia's daughter, too. He didn't like the idea of leaving the kid behind, even though he disliked children. It was a circular argument and made his head hurt.

The brass bell tinkled at the front of the store and interrupted Doyle's thoughts.

"Welcome to Fun Time," Tabitha said. "Is there anything..." her voice trailed off.

"Anyone else in here with you?" a man with a deep, commanding voice asked.

"Just me," Tabitha said, "and you. One lone officer out on a beat."

"What's that?" the cop asked.

"Nothing. Just saying the two of us don't make for a lot of witnesses."

The cop's voice filled with suspicion. "You been in trouble before?"

"Oh, my parents are always on me about something."

"Uh-huh."

Doyle glanced back at the Yeti costume. It reeked like garbage. He wondered if the helmet smelled worse than stale Fritos now.

"You see these two?" the cop asked. Doyle imagined the cop holding up the pictures of him and Macklin.

"Is that a trick question?" Tabitha asked.

"You getting smart?"

"College at night. Thank you for noticing."

"Huh?" the cop asked.

Doyle wanted to peek around the corner but was afraid of moving the storeroom door and calling attention to it.

"Those guys work here," Tabitha said. "That one is Doyle, and I don't know the name of the other guy. He's new."

"Doyle, huh?"

"That's right. Why are you looking for them?"

The cop hesitated before responding. "They won a prize."

"From the police department?"

"You like getting smart, huh?"

"College isn't for everyone," Tabitha said.

"How's that?"

"I was just wondering," she said, "what kind of prize the police department gives out?"

"Keep talking and you'll find out."

"No, thank you. You can give the prize to them."

Another pause. "What's in the back?"

Doyle moved toward the exit door. If he burst out now, he had no idea who would be on the other side. If the cop didn't catch Doyle, his buddies would know where he was. Maybe they would assume it had been Macklin in the storeroom. Regardless, more officers would assemble in the area and give chase.

Instead of running, Doyle could fight the cop. There was no guarantee how that would turn out, but Doyle believed he could disable the officer. Those weren't the thoughts of a better man, but if the cop was working with the Outfit, he brought the trouble on himself.

"Only supplies," Tabitha said, "but you're welcome to look. Don't knock anything over. It's all stacked sort of haphazardly back there. We're in the middle of inventory."

Another bit of silence. Doyle put his hand on the exit door and prepared to run. He wouldn't fight a cop. At least, not now.

"Never mind," the officer said. "If you see either of these guys, call the administration building."

"For their prize."

"That's right, smart mouth."

"Thank you for visiting," Tabitha said. "Enjoy your day at Fun Time."

"What is it with you people?"

A moment later, the brass bell rang once more.

"You can come out," Tabitha called. "He's gone."

Doyle left the safety of the storeroom.

Outside the business, several cops gathered. They chatted briefly, then moved away.

"What was that about?" Tabitha asked.

"A misunderstanding."

"Looks like a pretty big misunderstanding."

When the cops wandered further down Wonder Alley, Doyle approached the front of the store. "What's with the Yeti costume?" he asked.

She grinned. "I felt bad for it sitting out in the trash bin, so I rescued it. Why? Did it give you a scare?"

"Hardly."

"Uh-huh. Are you going to take it back?"

"No."

"You think I can keep it?"

He shrugged as he scanned The Pathway of Fun.

"You must be in trouble if you risked dumping that costume. It's Fun Time legend."

Doyle looked back at her. "Why didn't you tell that cop I was back there?"

"Because he was dirty," Tabitha said.

"How do you know?"

"They're all dirty." Her head bobbled. "You know how it is in other places? There are some good cops and some bad cops, but most of them are middle-of-the-road clock punchers? Kind of like everyone else in life?"

"I guess."

"That's not how it is here. All the cops are corrupt."

"Then why do you stay?"

"Because I like the weather."

Doyle leaned to get a better look out the window.

"You must not have known about all the corruption before you moved here."

"It caught me totally by surprise," Doyle said.

"Are you going to stick around?"

Doyle's eyes narrowed. "Not a chance."

He opened the door, and the bell tinkled. He stepped onto The Pathway of Fun.

"You still owe me for the T-shirt and shorts!" Tabitha hollered after him.

***

Doyle detoured to the fence line near the main entrance. The flow of guests entering the park had slowed to a trickle. It was late in the day, so the only ones entering now were those with annual passes. They could come and go throughout the year, ride one or two of the features, then leave. Doyle had worked at the amusement park for several weeks now and had become familiar with the process.

A dozen police cars clustered near the entrance. Behind them, a group of men in suits stood together, smoking cigarettes. They laughed in the nervous way men do before going into battle.

Doyle knew what this was. The Outfit was queueing its men for the after-hours push.

Whatever the marshals had planned, he doubted they would make it in time. He hoped Agent Ekleberry would come through.

Chapter 17

Doyle ducked behind some thick, flowering shrubs and watched the administration building.

Men in Hawaiian shirts moved in and out of the squat structure. A handful of cops stood outside. Their eyes darted about the park. Only a few words were exchanged. They meant business, and that business was locating Doyle and Macklin.

The Pathway of Fun was less than ten feet from him. Even though this part of the park was filled only with restaurants, many families still came through here, as it served as a shortcut of sorts. An attendee could walk past the administration building and the various sit-down eateries and avoid the little kid congestion that always occurred near Wonder Alley.

If any of the park's guests were paying attention, they could determine something nefarious was going on back here. Yet most families walked by, blissfully unaware a criminal organization had just kidnapped someone inside the park. Husbands grumbled to themselves as they studied theme park maps while wives struggled to herd untethered children that ran wild.

Did no one notice the open corruption at the administration building? Or did they just accept it as a normal day-to-day activity?

Overhead, a speaker crackled. *"Beauregard Smith, we know you can hear this. Your girlfriend and her kid are waiting for you at the administration building. Don't disappoint them by not showing up soon. Get here toot sweet."*

Unfortunately for Sophia and Taylor, they had broken away from their field trip group long before. Those folks wouldn't realize something terrible had happened to their friends. The group could finish their day at Fun Time and be none the wiser about the mother and daughter's plight. Even if they knew something happened, would they do anything about it?

Was the whole town complicit because they were afraid to stand up to the Outfit?

A little boy ran over to the bushes near where Doyle hid. He squatted lower, and the kid stood on his tiptoes. The child was likely six years old and wore an *I Survived the Terror* T-shirt. He spread apart the bushes closest to him.

"Jedi!" a father called. "Come here."

"Aw."

"Now."

The boy returned to his regular height and looked over his shoulder. "But there's something in the bushes."

Doyle dropped to his hands and knees. He couldn't see anything now. From behind him, some music played, and roller coasters clacked down their tracks. Happy screams filled the air.

"It's probably a snake," the father said. He sounded closer now, probably at the edge of the landscaped area. "Leave it alone."

Doyle cocked his head. He hadn't considered the possibility of snakes. He wasn't particularly scared of them, but he had a healthy respect for the reptile. His ears strained to pick up the sound of rattling or slithering.

Was it possible to hear a slithering snake?

Doyle scanned the surrounding ground.

"It wasn't a snake," the boy said. "It was a person."

"Jedi, what have I told you about making up stories?"

"I'm not."

Doyle prepared to run if the father yelled for the cops.

"Okay, buddy. I understand. It wasn't a snake. Why don't we get a funnel cake, and you can tell me all about the man who lives in the bushes?"

"But it's true," Jedi whined.

"I know," the father said. It sounded as if they were walking away. "That's why I want you to tell me all about it."

Doyle stayed low for some time. He worried perhaps the kid's interest might have inspired a cop or an Outfit man to check out what he was looking at.

He thought about backing out of the bushes. Perhaps this wasn't the smartest way to spy on the administration building. Although it gave him the best angle to watch it. He'd been there for several minutes before the kid spotted him. Maybe it was just dumb luck no one else had.

Doyle pushed himself into a squat and braved another look. Nothing had changed near the administration building. Right now, Doyle had two problems—rescue the mother and daughter and cause some mayhem for the Outfit.

This situation would have been so much easier for the man Doyle had been. The bookkeeper would have left Sophia and Taylor and simply picked an exit. That man would have blasted his way out and gone about his life.

The bushes rustled behind him. It was too big to be a snake.

Had the Outfit found him? Were the cops onto him? Had the kid convinced his father to investigate his discovery?

Doyle spun, prepared to fight. He didn't even consider pulling the gun from his waistband.

"Whoa," Macklin whispered. "Take it easy." He lifted his hands in a calming manner.

"What are you doing here?" Doyle asked.

"I figured you would show up sooner or later."

"Why's that?"

"Because the Outfit keeps calling for some Beauregard guy to come to the administration building." Macklin moved forward and hunched. "You got a good view from here." He glanced sideways at Doyle. "I did some thinking."

Doyle's expression remained flat.

"Someone must've put you in the Witness Protection Program and changed your name."

Macklin's attention returned to the administration building. "Although even if you weren't in the program, I would have changed that name, too. Beauregard."

Several seconds passed before Doyle asked, "What's wrong with it?"

"It's fine, I suppose, if you grew up on a farm in the 1920s. You must've gotten into a lot of fights as a kid."

"Some."

"I'll bet."

Doyle considered Macklin. "What happened to your bag?"

"Don't worry about it. It's someplace safe."

"What are you doing here?" Doyle asked.

"Thought you might like some company."

Doyle knew this was a lie. Earlier Macklin was upset when he learned Doyle had turned informant against the Satan's Dawgs. Showing up now meant the man had an ulterior motive.

Macklin eyed him. "You see the cops walking around with your picture and mine?"

"What about it?"

"The Outfit has better resources than I remembered." Macklin leaned forward as he watched some movement near the administration building. "What's your girlfriend like?"

An image of Daphne Winterbourne entered Doyle's mind. He glanced at Macklin. "I don't have a girlfriend."

"Then who's this person the Outfit is dangling as a lure?"

"A woman I met today."

Macklin studied Doyle. "You move fast."

"It's not like that," Doyle said.

Macklin winked. "Sure, it's not. She must be something special if you're willing to risk everything to get them free."

Doyle waved him off.

"All right, then. Tell me what it's like."

"You don't want to hear it."

"Don't do that. Tell me. I want to know why a guy in the protection program would risk everything for a woman and kid he doesn't know."

"Because it's something the guy I used to be would never do."

Macklin's smile was cruel. "Seeking redemption through acts of courage?"

Doyle studied the administration building again. The cops exchanged some words and moved toward the small structure. The guys in Hawaiian shirts gathered with them.

"Listen," Macklin continued. "I don't know what you did when you were in the life and, frankly, I don't care. You ratted, and that's the worst crime in the book."

"If that's the case, why are you here?"

"If you haven't paid attention, I'm stuck in here, too. We've only got a few hours left before the park closes and they come hunting for us. The best option is work together."

"Things are already in motion," Doyle said.

"By your friends in the government?"

He nodded. "I don't know how long it will take."

"They're not going to help me."

"Probably true."

"So what are we doing until then?"

"Rescuing a mother and daughter and creating general mayhem."

"Escape isn't at the top of the list?"

"Not until they're free."

The two men watched the administration building.

Macklin's gaze narrowed. "It's going to be impossible to get in there."

"Then we need to get everyone to come out, to abandon the building."

"What're you thinking?"

"I have an idea," Doyle said, "but it's not great." He quickly laid out his plan.

Macklin grimaced. "Sounds flimsy."

"It's better than your Yeti in a trash can stunt."

"That plan worked."

"So will mine."

Doyle turned to leave the shrubs, but Macklin grabbed his arm.

"Mind if I give you some advice?"

"Can we do this elsewhere?" Doyle jerked a thumb in the administration's direction. "We're pushing our luck in these bushes."

"It's as good a time as any," Macklin said.

Doyle dropped to a knee. "What is it?"

"In this game," Macklin said, "you can't have anything others can leverage you with."

"I understand that."

"No girlfriend. No kids."

Even though Macklin was talking about Sophia, Daphne Winterbourne came immediately to mind. She was the woman he couldn't stop thinking about. He reluctantly said, "I get it."

"The partners I use on any job know the rules. If one of us gets caught, we're on our own. No rats."

Doyle started to protest, but Macklin lifted a hand to stop him. "That's not what this is about."

"Feels like it is," Doyle said.

"There are no friends in this business. If people say they're your friends, they're lying." Macklin cocked his head. "Get it?"

"That's it?" Doyle asked. "This is your advice?"

Doyle already knew these rules. He had lived his life like this when he was with the Satan's Dawgs. No permanent attachments. Surface-only friendships. In the end, every man was for himself. However, he didn't want to live like that anymore.

"Just so we're clear," Macklin said, "we're not friends."

"If that's how you want it to be."

"This is your last chance to walk away without the woman and her kid."

"I won't do that," Doyle said. "They're in this trouble because of me. They don't deserve it." As an afterthought, Doyle said, "And you don't have to help."

"If it's an opportunity to hurt the Outfit, you can count me in." Macklin checked out the administration building one more time. "Besides, we're not getting out of here if we don't work together. If getting you as my partner means I've got to help save some random mother and daughter—" He shrugged. "It goes against my better judgment, but maybe it will help my karma."

Doyle tapped the man's arm with the back of his hand. "Let's go find a golf cart."

***

Avoiding the watchful eyes of Outfit men and corrupt cops was challenging when Doyle was on his own. It became slightly easier with Macklin since they could watch each other's back.

Macklin didn't share the same sentiment. "This was simpler when I was on my own."

They didn't move militarily, leapfrogging from one place of concealment to the next. That type of activity would draw too much attention from the park attendees. The two men didn't brazenly walk down the middle of The Pathway of Fun like they were in the climactic scene of some western film. That would have been stupid.

Instead, Doyle and Macklin walked shoulder to shoulder, their heads swiveling constantly. With Doyle in his Hawaiian shirt and Macklin in his plaid shirt, they looked like two fathers searching for a lost child.

"Did you like being a janitor?" Macklin asked. "Just making conversation. You don't have to answer if you don't want to. I don't care."

"I'm a custodian."

Macklin rolled his eyes. "You're playing word games."

"Custodians look after properties while janitors only clean them."

"Listen to you." Macklin shook his head. "You sound like a recruiting poster."

"It's an honest living."

"You were pretending to do a job just like me."

"You did it for one day. I've been here for three weeks." Doyle scanned the nearby crowd. "It was a good gig."

"There's no way you enjoyed picking up garbage." Macklin walked backward now so he could get a better look at Doyle. "How could you have?"

"My grandmother used to say, 'One man's trash is another man's treasure.'"

"Spare me. That saying makes no sense. In the end, it's still a pile of trash, no matter how much the guy is loving it."

Doyle began to explain how he liked the peacefulness of his job, but up ahead he saw three goons in Hawaiian shirts. They were looking in the opposite direction. He grabbed Macklin and said, "The Outfit."

Macklin stopped and turned. The two men hurried into the nearest store. The Candy

Shop's brass bell playfully tinkled above them as they entered.

A tall, pimply teenager, Doyle knew as Gavin stood behind the counter. Two Lindo Gato cops stood across from him. The older of the pair—a fat, jowly man who wheezed loudly—angrily flapped two photographs as if he were trying to fan out a fire. The younger officer—a tanned muscular man who seemed slightly unhinged—ate colorful pieces of candy that he cupped in his hand.

Overhead, "Sugar, Sugar" played through speakers hanging from the ceiling.

As if in slow motion, the clerk pointed at Doyle and Macklin. Both cops faced them. The jowly cop still held the pictures outward.

A long second passed, and no one dared move. Doyle wondered what would happen if they backed out right then.

Macklin said, "I'll take the fat one." He rapidly took three steps and leaped into the air.

"Gah," the older cop said and stepped backward.

The younger cop threw his handful of candy at Doyle, then reached for his gun. Doyle jumped on him and grabbed him by the shirt. Before the officer could remove his weapon, Doyle swung him around and tossed him into a display of gumballs. A vibrant waterfall cascaded to the ground amid exploding glass.

Behind Doyle, the sounds of a struggle resulted in another crash.

Gavin's fingers slipped into his blond hair and his eyes widened with shock.

The younger cop rose to his knee and frantically reached for his gun. "You're not getting out of here, rat."

Doyle stepped forward and punched him across the chin. The cop stiffened and fell into another display rack filled with various flavors of licorice. The shelves collapsed, and the jars tumbled to the ground.

Overhead, the song on the radio changed to the 1980s song, "I Want Candy." Doyle didn't know who sang it.

He frowned as he studied the unconscious police officer. Hitting a cop was not the action of a better man, far from it. Flashes of his dark days appeared in his mind like an unwelcome guest. Then he remembered this cop was working for the Outfit. He wasn't one of the good guys.

The good guys, Doyle thought dryly. *What happened to me?*

He turned.

Macklin stood there with a gun in his hand. "That was fun."

Doyle lifted his chin toward the heavy-set cop. He lay crumbled on the ground. "How's your guy?"

"Alive. He wasn't much of a fighter. Yours?"

Doyle shrugged. "It went quick."

Gavin's hands were still clasped in his golden locks, and his eyes traveled about the store, taking the damage in.

Nothing escaped the melee except the counter. Most of the glass jars were broken, and colorful bits of flotsam and jetsam were strewn about.

Doyle said, "We're sorry about the mess."

The clerk slowly shook his head. "I've waited months for a moment like this."

"You have?"

Gavin's eyes focused, and he glanced at both men. "How could you miss all the puns?"

Doyle and Macklin looked at each other.

The clerk's fingers left his hair and dragged down his face. "This place is full of them." He eyed Macklin. "You should have said 'That was sweet' instead of 'That was fun.'"

Macklin frowned. "I don't pun."

"Or you—" Gavin looked to Doyle. "It went quick? How about 'Like taking candy from a baby?'"

Doyle frowned. "I don't pun either."

"Neither of you even said 'Trick or treat' when you hit those cops." Gavin tossed his hands into the air. "That one was so obvious."

Doyle looked at Macklin, then jerked his head toward the door. "Let's go."

"Or how about shouting 'Payday' when you clobbered those guys?" Gavin said. "So easy."

Macklin moved toward the counter. The gun dangled by his side.

"Relax," Doyle said.

"Those were funny," Gavin said. "C'mon. No Snickers for those puns?" He grinned broadly.

Macklin's expression flattened, and he raised a fist. "How about I knock you out?"

"Wanna give me a Whopper, huh?" Gavin playfully punched himself in the chin.

Macklin grabbed for the clerk, but the younger man jumped back from the counter.

Gavin said, "You're just mad because you've missed so many."

"Stop pushing your luck," Doyle said. He moved to the window to ensure the pathway was free of cops and Outfit goons.

"How's it look?" Macklin asked.

Doyle looked over his shoulder. "Clear."

Macklin pointed menacingly at Gavin. "Don't call anyone for a few minutes. Got it?"

"Why would I do that?" The clerk spread his arms wide. "This has been the most fun I've had in my whole life." Gavin's eyes twinkled with mischief.

Macklin's lip curled. "Whatever you're thinking—don't. I'm warning you."

The clerk put his hand over his heart. "I sincerely can't say thank you enough."

Macklin looked over his shoulder at Doyle, then back to Gavin. His face relaxed, and he nodded. "You're welcome."

"It really mint a lot."

Macklin's face reddened. "I hate you."

"Seeing this go down meant more than all the stars in the Milky Way."

"Forget him," Doyle said. "Let's go."

Macklin shook his head twice, then headed for the exit. "I'm about to hurt that guy."

"You really want a Pez of me, huh?"

Macklin stopped walking. His shoulders hunched around his ears. He closed his eyes and his face purpled.

"You're pushing it, kid," Doyle said. "I'd suggest giving it a rest."

Gavin laughed. "I'm sorry. I'm just a Nerd for jokes."

Macklin lifted his gun.

The clerk lifted his hands into the air. "All right, all right. I'll stop."

"Yeah, you will," Macklin said. "Or I'll make sure you stop permanently."

Doyle pushed down on the barrel of Macklin's gun. "Everybody take a deep breath."

Gavin squinted and turned his head away.

Macklin put the gun into his pocket. "Your customer service is the worst."

Gavin nodded. "So I've been told."

Doyle went to the door and the brass bell tinkled. He popped his head out and searched for Hawaiian shirts and uniforms on The Pathway of Fun. He stepped out and Macklin followed.

"I don't get you," Macklin said. "One moment you're smacking a cop, the next you're worried about scaring a clerk. What's up with that?"

"I'm a complicated guy," Doyle said.

"Tell me about it."

Doyle headed deeper into the park.

Chapter 18

A Fun Time speaker buzzed before another announcement. *"Beauregard Smith, your girlfriend and her kid are getting impatient. Don't disappoint them. Bring along your partner while you're at it."*

Macklin eyed Doyle. "They're grasping at straws."

Doyle shook his head. "The only leverage they've got is Sophia and her kid."

"They'll push on it until it breaks."

That's what Doyle expected, and it was why he needed to get the woman and her child free.

Doyle and Macklin located a golf cart operated by a tandem of Fun Time security guards. Artie and Flint ate ice cream cones and watched The Palomino slowly spin.

"I'll take the dumb looking one," Macklin said.

Doyle didn't bother asking which one he meant. "No. We won't hurt them."

Macklin frowned. "Why not?"

"Because I know them."

"Then how are we going to get it?"

"We're going to ask to use it."

Macklin cocked his head. "And if they say no?"

"We'll figure out another way."

"Who died and made you boss?"

"Park policy."

"You don't work for the park anymore."

"It's my plan, and I say we aren't hurting them."

Macklin rolled his eyes. "Some plan."

No Outfit goons or police officers were near the two guards. As Doyle and Macklin approached the cart, the two security men turned to them with lopsided smiles.

Artie sat behind the steering wheel and licked a cone topped with blue ice cream. Flint's treat was purple.

"Hey, fellas," Artie said. His blue lips broadened in a smile. "The line at The Terror is crazy long. You should see it."

Flint's purple tongue peeked out between his lips, and he giggled. "Two Yangos for the price of one."

Artie giggled. "I'm seeing double."

Macklin jerked a thumb over his shoulder. "Outta the cart, hopheads."

Doyle moved closer. "What my friend meant to say was—"

"Now," Macklin growled.

Flint slid out of his seat. "Geez, dude, what'd we do?"

"Yeah, fellas." Artie bit into his ice cream. "What'd we do?"

Macklin dropped into the passenger seat. "Give us your walkie-talkies."

Flint licked his ice cream and stared at his partner.

Artie pointed his cone at Macklin. "If we do that, we'll get in trouble."

Doyle dropped behind the steering wheel. "What Macklin is trying to say is—"

"*Now.*" Macklin snapped his fingers and pointed at Flint.

The guard continued to lick his cone as he unhooked the walkie-talkie from his belt and handed it over. "Not cool."

Artie shrugged and unhooked his walkie-talkie. He also gave it to Macklin. "We'd appreciate if you didn't tell anybody about this."

Macklin smacked Doyle's arm. "Enough with the pleasantries. This is a heist. Let's go."

Doyle dropped the golf cart into reverse and zoomed backward for several feet. Then he hit the brakes. He flipped the lever forward, and the cart sped away.

***

"Where we headed?" Macklin asked.

"To get a diversion," Doyle said.

"I thought the golf cart was the diversion."

Doyle waved a hand. "Only the first part."

He jerked the wheel and Macklin grabbed the support rail to stop himself from falling out. Doyle narrowly avoided Freddy the Frog.

"Hey!" the Frog yelled. "Everyone's looking for you!" His voice trailed off behind them.

"Hand me one of those radios," Doyle said.

Macklin pointed to a cluster of police officers up ahead. "Cops," he said and slid down in his seat. It was a pointless action since there was no dashboard to hide behind in a golf cart.

Doyle spun the steering wheel and ducked into an alley between a couple of vendor shops. When he cleared the back, he turned behind a building and stopped.

Macklin pushed up in his seat and held out a walkie-talkie. Doyle took it and keyed the microphone.

"Ainsley," he said.

In a moment, she responded, "*Who is this?*"

"Your friend."

"*How'd you get on this channel?*"

"The goofballs loaned us their walkie-talkies. Can anyone else listen in?"

"*Maybe,*" she said. "*This is the security channel, but we're the only ones working today.*"

"Did you ever hear from my friend?"

"*I did. He said sit tight. Things are in motion.*"

Doyle didn't know if Ekleberry had been cryptic for Ainsley's benefit or if she was being ambiguous because she was broadcasting on the radio. Either way, it told him enough. The FBI was on the way. And Mr. Gilbert had spoken with the marshal's hotline, and they told him help was also on the way. Pretty soon, Lone Star Family Fun Time was going to be crawling with federal agents.

He pressed the transmit button again. "Remember that place I left you?"

"*How could I forget?*"

"Meet us there."

"*Copy.*"

A thought occurred to Doyle. "And if you can find Oskar, bring him with you."

He held the radio for a couple of seconds longer, expecting her to respond. When Ainsley didn't, Doyle handed the walkie-talkie back to Macklin.

"Wanna tell me what we're doing?"

"We're picking up Yango," Doyle said.

"In case you forgot, we threw him away."

"Yango never dies." Doyle lifted a hand from the steering wheel. "He came back from the dead."

Macklin cocked his head. "So now he's a zombie?"

Chapter 19

Doyle burst into the Happy Hour Shop. Macklin was close behind. The brass bell clanged when they entered.

"Welcome to Fun Time—" Tabitha looked up from her book and her eyes narrowed. "Nerts. It's you two."

"We need to go into the storeroom," Doyle said.

"Of course, you do."

Macklin nodded as they passed Tabitha.

"You two sure caused a lot of trouble today," she said.

"It wasn't intentional," Macklin said.

Tabitha dropped her attention back to her book. "Could have fooled me."

When they reached the storeroom, Doyle motioned for the door. "After you."

Macklin frowned. He twisted the knob and stepped in. He didn't jump at the sight of the Yeti costume draped over the boxes. "Cute," he said. He looked over his shoulder. "You knew this was here?"

Doyle pushed into the storeroom. He handed the Yeti helmet to Macklin.

"Yango's like a bad cold," Macklin said. "We can't seem to get rid of him."

Doyle gathered up the rest of the costume. "Let's go."

As they passed through the store's lobby, Tabitha looked up. "Hey, where are you going with my costume??"

"We need it," Doyle said.

"But you said I could have it."

He paused in front of the counter. "It's important."

She crossed her arms. "You threw him away. I rescued him. Possession is nine-tenths of the law."

Macklin stepped forward. "Doyle's in possession of it now so you can take your one-tenth and stuff it."

Tabitha's eyes widened. "But I rescued it."

Doyle softened his expression. "I'm sorry about my friend."

Macklin turned to him. "You're what?"

"And you're right," Doyle said to Tabitha. "I threw the costume away, and you found it. I shouldn't have taken Yango without asking."

Suspicion filled her eyes. "What are you going to do with him?"

"Create a diversion."

Macklin threw his hands in the air. "You don't need to explain anything. Let's get out of here!"

Tabitha nodded. "Well, thank you for recognizing you took him without asking."

Doyle lifted the costume. "I'd really like to use it."

"I guess Yango was never really mine to begin with." She waved a hand. "Go ahead. Take him."

"Finally," Macklin muttered. "Can we go?"

Doyle headed toward the door.

"But don't forget, you still owe me for the T-shirt and shorts!"

Outside, Doyle put the costume and paws into the basket on the golf cart. Macklin stuffed the helmet on top, then turned to scan The Pathway of Fun.

"Sure seems quiet all of a sudden," he said.

"Yeah," Doyle agreed.

Families ebbed and flowed on the pathway, but no men in Hawaiian shirts were in the mix and the cops seemed to have disappeared as well. Music and happy screams from the rollercoasters filled the air.

"What's happened?" Macklin asked.

"I don't know, but I've got a bad feeling."

The two men climbed into the golf cart.

***

As the two drove, Macklin twisted in his seat and scanned the park. "Still nothing."

"We'll get them to come back out soon enough."

"You think this is going to work?"

Doyle yanked the steering wheel, and the golf cart zipped between a couple of buildings. The little vehicle bounced and jounced its way around bushes and trees until it arrived at a small shack. Doyle drove around the back in hopes of hiding it from any unwanted eyes. He hopped out and ran to its rear.

Macklin looked around. "What is this place?"

"A maintenance shed," Doyle said. He grabbed the Yeti helmet and hurried to the door. "Grab the rest of the suit."

As before, the small building was unlocked. Doyle hurried inside and flicked on the lights. He tossed the Abominable Snowman's head onto the table.

When Macklin entered, he stopped and silently appreciated it. Doyle shut the door, took the remaining costume pieces from him, and set them onto the table.

Macklin's brow furrowed. "Maintenance shed, huh? So the park has maintenance guys? I've never seen any of them."

"Me neither, but I guess they're out there." Doyle moved to the speaker system next to the phone. "This is the last piece of our diversion."

"You want to provide an update to the families? How's that going to help?"

Doyle shook his head. "We're going to close Fun Time early."

"What for?"

"So everyone will start flowing to the exits at the same time."

Macklin lifted his hands in mock surrender. "Hold on. If we get all these guests to leave, what's stopping the Outfit and their friends from coming in?"

"That's what we want."

"That's what we want?" Macklin's eyes bulged. "Are you listening to yourself? They'll steamroll us."

"I've got that covered."

"With what?" He pointed at the dirty Yeti costume. "We already tried that. It's not going to work a second time, especially not with the whole Outfit barreling down on us. You need help with your diversions."

"Diversions really aren't my specialty."

"What is?"

"Breaking things."

Macklin lifted an eyebrow. "Were you some sort of enforcer?"

Doyle shook his head. "I was a bookkeeper."

"A bookkeeper?" Macklin spun in a circle. "My freedom is tied to the escape plan put together by an accountant? I'm out of here."

"Hold on. We want the Outfit to bring all their men at the same time. It's going to help us."

Macklin was about to ask a question when gravel crunched outside the maintenance shop. It sounded as if a couple of golf carts had arrived. Macklin hunched and pulled his gun from his waistband.

"Easy," Doyle said.

The door opened and Ainsley stepped inside. When she saw Macklin's gun, her hands went into the air.

Macklin eyed Doyle. "This is the one you called for help?"

Oskar bounded into the building. He stepped from behind Ainsley and said, "This better be good, Flanders." His eyes widened and his arms shot upward. "Heavens to Betsy!"

Macklin's gun rolled forward in his hand and his eyes darkened. "You're kidding me."

The custodial manager lowered his arms. "Don't judge me, tough guy. It's clear you didn't read the employee handbook. There's no swearing inside the park."

It was one of the many policies Doyle liked about working at Fun Time—employees could be fired for cussing. Doyle's grandmother taught him foul language was the first sign of a weak mind. Even in high school, when his friends were experimenting with the various ways to offend adults, Doyle took no interest in profanity.

The Dawgs thought Doyle was odd for never cursing. Even his habit of knitting to relieve stress—another Ma lesson—was overlooked by the club. The Dawgs forgave many behaviors they thought strange because they valued intimidation and retribution—abilities Doyle used to be very skilled at.

"It's not like the folks out there haven't heard a bad word in their lives," Macklin said.

Oskar put his hands on his hips and jutted his chin out. "I don't care if they've heard them all. If you work for the park, you don't have a potty mouth."

"In case you forgot, I no longer work here."

The maintenance supervisor nodded. "Well, in that case, stick it in your ear, buddy."

Macklin smirked. "Good one. You're really flirting with the line there."

Ainsley pushed the door closed. "What's with the gun? You guys asked us here."

"He's being cautious," Doyle said.

Her face pinched. "He's being a jerk is what he's being."

"Yeah," Oskar said. "What she said."

Macklin shoved the gun back into his waistband. "It's who I am."

"What are we doing here?" Ainsley asked.

"We're rescuing a mother and a daughter, then we're getting out of the park."

Oskar opened his mouth to say something, but Ainsley cut him off by holding up her hand in front of his face.

"Wait," she said, "Just exactly *who* are we rescuing?"

"You've met them," Doyle said.

Ainsley's eyes widened. "Oh my God, not her! Why are we saving that woman? She's horrible."

Both Macklin and Oskar crossed their arms and stared at Ainsley.

Doyle patted the air with a hand. "Relax."

"Don't tell me to relax, Doyle."

"The Outfit grabbed them because they think she's my girlfriend."

"But she's not." Ainsley's face reddened. "She doesn't even know your real name. She called you Yango."

Macklin's and Oskar's heads bounced between the two.

Ainsley blinked repeatedly. "Not that I even care."

Doyle said, "We're rescuing them because it's the right thing to do."

"There you go, kid," Oskar said. "I knew I liked you."

Ainsley tsked. "The right thing is for Doyle to get himself to safety."

Macklin nodded. "That's what I think. One hundred percent."

She pointed. "See, Doyle? You should let your friends in the FBI handle it."

Macklin stiffened. "The FBI?"

Doyle held up his hand. "Everything is going to be okay. Trust me."

Oskar furrowed his brow. "How do you know people in the FBI?"

"It's a long story," Doyle said. He turned to Ainsley. "What exactly did Ekleberry say?"

"He said sit tight," Ainsley said, "things are in motion."

"Did he say for how long?"

She shook her head. "No. Just sit tight. That's it."

So she hadn't been cryptic on the walkie-talkie. That's just the way the FBI agent had spoken.

"What's an Ekleberry?" Oskar asked. He turned to Macklin. "Do you know?"

Macklin dismissively flicked away the man's question. He moved closer to Doyle. "How friendly are you with this FBI agent?"

"I know him," Doyle said. "But we don't have beers together."

"I guess what I'm asking is, do I have to worry about you serving me up to them?"

"For what?" Doyle asked. "I don't even know what you've done. I barely know you."

"Let's keep it that way, Mr. Friends-with-Feds." Macklin stepped back.

Ainsley put her hands on her hips. "Will somebody explain why we're here?"

"Oskar," Doyle said, "I need you to do something you're going to hate."

"What's that?"

Doyle picked up the Yeti helmet. "I need you to wear a costume."

"And be one of them prima donnas? Not on your life!"

***

"I look ridiculous in this thing," Oskar said.

"No, you don't," Doyle said.

Macklin chuckled. "Yes, he does."

Oskar turned left and right like a stiff-armed robot. "Why's it smell like an old dog?"

Ainsley shook her head. "Yango looks like he fell in that *Star Wars* trash compactor. Chewbacca wore it better."

But Oskar was right. He didn't even have the helmet on yet and he looked foolish. The costume was too big on him. The arm fabric hung beyond his hands and the leg fabric draped far below his knees. They didn't have the Yeti boots, so Oskar still wore his shoes. Doyle had not accounted for the dramatic difference in height.

For his part in the plan, Oskar would only sit in the golf cart, so the suit didn't have to fit perfectly, but this was too much.

220

Oskar waved his arms and the fabric flapped. "Look at me. I'm about to fly away."

"Take it off," Doyle said.

"Great. I didn't like what you had in mind for me."

Macklin and Ainsley lifted the Abominable Snowman's chest portion over Oskar's head. They plopped it onto the table.

Doyle grabbed a set of shears from the corner. "Take off the pants, too."

Oskar watched Doyle. "So, I'm still wearing the suit?"

"It's part of the plan." Doyle cut off a chunk of fabric from one arm with the pruning shears. It wasn't a clean cut and left an irregular jagged edge.

"The plan," the custodial manager muttered. "The well-thought-out plan."

Oskar tugged the pants off. He had pulled them over his own clothing. The costume was that much bigger than he was. Macklin tossed the bottoms onto the table next to where Doyle worked.

Ainsley moved closer. "Mr. Gilbert is going to have a fit when he sees what you did to the costume. He's always going on about how the Yango suit was an antique and it's an honor for whoever gets to wear it."

Doyle shrugged. "He knows it was in the trash can."

"But he probably could have gotten the stains out." Ainsley cringed when Doyle snipped the final bit of fabric from the second arm. "That's gonna be hard to ignore."

"Put it on." Doyle pushed the snowman's chest across the table.

"I'm not a performing monkey," Oskar said.

"You are today." Macklin hefted the section of costume and lifted it above Oskar's head. "Want a banana?" He tugged the chest portion in place on Oskar.

The custodial manager stuck his arms out wide. The fabric stopped perfectly at his right wrist. On his left, though, the fabric went up to his forearm. "You might have cut a little deep, kid."

"It's fine," Doyle said. "You'll be able to drive now."

"I look like a hand-me-down toy."

Macklin snickered. "You wish you looked that good."

Doyle cut some fabric from the first leg of the costume. "Since we've got time, is everybody clear on their part of the plan?"

"It's not rocket science," Ainsley said. "Do you think it'll work?"

"It's going to create a lot of commotion."

"What happens if it doesn't work?"

Doyle looked up. "The Outfit gets its hands on us." He lopped off the final piece of fabric on the Yeti bottoms and pushed them across the table. "Give them a go."

Oskar pulled the pants on. Just like the uppers, one leg fit perfectly. The second was cut halfway up a shin.

"No one will notice," Doyle said. "And forget the paws. They'll be too big."

Doyle handed the Yeti helmet to Oskar. When he slid it on, he said, "It's hard to see anything in this."

"You'll be okay," Doyle said.

"Why's it smell like old corn chips in here?" Oskar lifted his arms above his head. "*Boo!* What do you think? Am I scary?"

Doyle thought he looked like a mashed potato, but he kept his thoughts to himself. He didn't want to damage Oskar's confidence. The man didn't like actors and already was hesitant to do this. He needed his self-esteem bolstered. "You look great."

Ainsley smirked. "The heck he does. He looks like the Yeti melted in the sun, then was thrown in a shady dumpster to cool down."

From behind the helmet, Oskar whimpered, "Aw."

Macklin snickered. "He looks like an albino version of Oscar the Grouch."

Doyle glanced at him.

"What?" Macklin shrugged. "I've seen *Sesame Street*. I was a kid once."

"That's it." Oskar took off the helmet. "I'm not doing this."

Doyle said, "You're the only one who can do it."

"Let Ainsley." The maintenance supervisor thrust the helmet toward her.

"She needs to be here, and you need to be out there."

"All right. Fine." Oskar frowned and stared at the helmet. "But just because the show must go on."

Chapter 20

Oskar as Yango the Yeti zoomed off in the golf cart. He honked as he went. *Beep. Beep beep.* The frenetic rhythm continued.

Doyle and Macklin followed him in the second cart.

"Is he playing a tune?" Macklin asked.

"'The Farmer in the Dell.'"

Macklin glanced at him. "You're kidding."

"Or 'Bloodbath in Paradise.'" Doyle shrugged. "I can't tell the difference with the way he's playing."

Oskar continued to bang on the horn. When he made The Pathway of Fun, he bounced into the middle. A group of attendees screamed and jumped out of the way. Oskar yanked the steering wheel and headed toward The Terror. A woman pulled her child closer, shook her fist at the rapidly departing cart, and shouted an expletive.

The Family Fun Time speaker sputtered. Doyle slowed the golf cart so he could hear the announcement.

"*Attention Fun Time guests,*" Ainsley said, "*due to unfortunate events, the park is closing immediately. Please move in an orderly fashion to the closest exit, where a refund will be given. We hope you've enjoyed your day.*"

Faces in the crowd registered confusion. Many looked at their spouses to see if they understood what was occurring.

Doyle grabbed his walkie-talkie and keyed it. "Ainsley, they're not reacting to your announcement. Do it again."

The speaker warbled as it came back to life. *"This is no joke, folks. Hop to it. Head to the exits now. Refunds are waiting. Come back and see us soon."*

"It's not working," Macklin said.

The crowd milled about. Many seemed confused by Ainsley's message since the attractions continued to operate. Several men in the crowd shrugged and motioned their families toward the nearest rides. It was clear they had no intention of leaving the park now.

Doyle's plan depended on confusion.

He expected some guests not to move toward the exits, but most ignored Ainsley's announcement. If they weren't motivated to get refunds, then there wouldn't be uprisings at the various exits. This wouldn't pull the Outfit's men and the dirty cops out of the entrenched positions from the administration building.

Oskar's driving about as Yango was supposed to add to some of that confusion. It had been some time since the Outfit had been looking for anyone in the costume, but Doyle hoped a Yango sighting might generate some interest.

All seemed for naught as the Fun Time customers ignored Ainsley's broadcast.

The park's speaker system warbled again. *"She's right,"* a male voice said. *"The park is closing now. Make your way to the exits, toot sweet. Forget about those refunds. Get out now."*

Doyle slowed the cart even further as he looked about. A male guest loudly complained to anyone who listened that he wanted a refund. His wife dutifully pointed out they would have gotten it had they left a few minutes earlier, like she suggested. No one paid them any attention as they burst into argument.

The park's rides continued to operate, and attendees waited in line. Most guests didn't seem bothered by the announcements, and no one hurried toward any of the exits.

Doyle stopped the cart.

"What's the holdup?" Macklin asked.

"If we arrive at the administration building early, there's going to be a welcoming party for us."

"We knew that."

"But we figured some of them would clear out to deal with the commotion."

Macklin smirked. "You figured that. I told you this wouldn't work. You should have left the distraction to me. Like you said, you're better at breaking stuff."

The walkie-talkie squelched. *"Doyle, did you hear that? The Outfit is trying to take credit for your idea."*

He keyed the microphone. "I don't care who takes credit as long as it works."

"Oh, I'll make it work."

The park's speaker system warbled. "*Move it, people!*" Ainsley said. "*You are in danger. This is not an exercise. Domestic terrorists in Hawaiian shirts have overrun the park.*"

Macklin grimaced. "That just upped the ante."

"*Get to the exits now!*" Ainsley continued. "*If you make it out alive, we look forward to seeing you again.*"

Several women in the crowd screamed. A man picked up his daughter and ran with her under his arm. She must have been heavier than expected because about ten feet later, he put her down. They walked hand-in-hand toward the nearest exit.

The park's speaker buzzed. "*Domestic terrorist is an unfair label,*" the male voice said. "*But to be fair, you are in danger. Get out now. No refunds.*"

"Are we gonna sit here all day," Macklin asked, "or we gonna put this brilliant plan of yours into action?"

Doyle stomped on the accelerator.

As he weaved through the crowd, men and women threw things at him. Most of the items were harmless, like stuffed animals resembling Yango the Yeti and Sassy Sasquatch. However, one teenager threw a half-eaten funnel cake. A bald man hurled a snow globe that exploded against the front of the cart. Several held their cameras up and recorded Doyle and Macklin careening by.

"Why are they throwing stuff at us?" Doyle asked.

Macklin turned to him and pulled back. "It's your shirt!"

Doyle had forgotten the garish orange and white shirt he was wearing.

The cart moved through an angry crowd of park attendees like a salmon swimming upstream. A hot dog splatted against the Plexiglas windshield, followed by a large cup of soda. Macklin flinched as a stuffed Freddy the Frog bounced against his shoulder.

"Grab the wheel," Doyle said.

When Macklin did, Doyle yanked the Hawaiian shirt apart and popped the buttons. He tugged it off his back and tossed the garment aside.

Up ahead, there were cops in the crowd. Their backs were to Doyle and Macklin. The officers held their arms in the air and shouted helpful things like, "No pushing," and "Single file!" The cops didn't notice the cart as it whisked behind them.

Outfit men in Hawaiian shirts hustled toward the administration building. However, they were beaten back by the Fun Time crowd. A goon in a Hawaiian shirt attempted to surrender to an approaching mob but was clubbed by a father carrying a snow globe.

Macklin grinned. "Why does a Texas theme park even have snow globes?"

The golf cart rounded the corner, and the crowd thinned out. As Doyle had hoped, no one now guarded the administration building. They raced forward. When the cart neared the building, Doyle jammed the brakes and spun the steering wheel. They skidded sideways to a stop.

Both men hopped out and drew their guns. They took two steps toward the administration building when the door popped open.

A heavy-set man stepped out. He had an arm around Sophia's neck and a gun poked into her waist. Behind them was Taylor.

"If it ain't the thorns in my side," Niccolò Esposito said.

Sophia's eyes widened when she saw Doyle. She enthusiastically waved. "You saved me! You really saved me!"

Taylor rolled her eyes. She muttered something, but Doyle was too far away to hear it.

The Outfit boss shook Sophia. "Ease up with that nonsense."

"But he's my hero."

"He ain't done nothing yet," Esposito said.

"Let her go," Doyle said unenthusiastically. The words dribbled out like cold molasses.

Macklin cast a sideways glance. "You wanna try that again?"

Doyle cleared his throat and waggled his gun. "Let them go," he said forcefully. He reminded himself that he was there to rescue the kid. The mother was an unfortunate byproduct of his chivalry.

"And give up my leverage?" Esposito asked. "You're outta your mind, rat." He pushed Sophia forward, and they walked down the steps.

"Your men are being overrun," Macklin said.

"They'll be back soon enough."

"The law is on the way," Doyle said.

The Outfit boss chuckled. "I own the law. Ain't you figured that out by now?"

"I mean the marshals and the FBI, too."

This seemed to confuse Esposito. He looked at Macklin. "You turning rat, too?"

"Not me," Macklin said.

"But you two are partners."

"Only for today and only because you made us." Macklin jerked his head to Doyle. "As soon as we walk out of here, I'll never see this guy again."

The boss nodded. "You and me, Macklin, we got unfinished business."

"Let the women go and we can finish it another day."

He jerked his head. "You two, move closer together."

"Not a chance," Macklin said.

"Let the kid go," Doyle said. "She didn't do anything to you."

Esposito looked at Taylor. "Go on. Disappear."

The girl looked at her mother.

"It's okay," Sophia said. She smiled bravely. "Make sure you say nice things about me."

Taylor ran over to Doyle.

The boss took his arm away from Sophia's throat. It disappeared behind her back for a moment. When it reappeared, there was a phone in it. He pressed a button and held it to his ear. "Yeah," Esposito said. "It's me. Get all the boys out of the park. You heard me right. The law is on the way. No, not that law, the fuzz. The Feds. Uh-huh. That's right. Get 'em out, toot sweet. We're leaving."

He hung up and put the phone away. "Just so we understand each other, Macklin. He gets the broad, and you get to run free until another day."

"Until another day," Macklin agreed.

The boss moved his gun away from Sophia's side. "Go get your man."

She hopped once, then skipped, then sprinted toward Doyle with her arms wide. "Yango!"

Doyle held up a hand. "I've got a girlfriend."

Sophia stopped in front of him. Her eyes traveled his length. "But you don't have your shirt on."

"So?"

"Yeah," Taylor said. "So?"

Sophia turned to her daughter. "That's the international symbol for romance, honey. It's on the covers of all the books. I'm not making this stuff up."

Esposito moved toward a golf cart parked near the administration building. He kept his gun trained on Macklin while Macklin pointed his weapon at the fat man. The two were locked in a game of chicken. Someone had to give first.

Finally, the boss swung into the golf cart and stomped on the accelerator.

Macklin lifted his gun and took aim at Esposito. Doyle put his hand on top of Macklin's gun and pushed down.

"What're you doing?" Macklin angrily asked.

"Not today," Doyle said. "We had a deal."

Macklin grunted. "Fine. But just because your family is here." He strode away.

"We're going to be a family," Sophia said excitedly as she reached for Doyle.

Taylor slipped in between the two. "Mom! Stop!"

Doyle stepped back.

"I don't want a theme park actor as my stepdad." She looked over her shoulder. "No offense."

Doyle shrugged. "None taken."

Taylor took her mom's hands. "I know you want to give me a good childhood and a regular dad again." She jerked her head toward Doyle. "Does this guy look like he can keep a job for more than a week?" Taylor looked over her shoulder. "Again, no offense."

Doyle's brow furrowed. "Some offense taken."

Sophia frowned. "I'm trying, Honey."

"You could probably do better than some guy covered in tattoos." Taylor looked over her shoulder. She opened her mouth, but Doyle said it for her.

"Yeah. I got it. No offense."

He hurried into the administration building, trading his new almost-family for his own shoes and his apartment key.

Chapter 21

Doyle tossed a green duffel bag onto the bed and unzipped it. He moved to the dresser and emptied the bottom drawer of his jeans and T-shirts. He hurriedly stuffed them into the bag and returned to the dresser. Next, he grabbed his socks and underwear and shoved them into the duffel.

He didn't have a lot of items to collect from his apartment. Not only had he been in Lindo Gato for just a few weeks, but his frequent moves since joining the Witness Protection Program had not allowed him to accumulate much. Basically, he had some clothes, a few paperbacks, a knitting kit, and a cat.

Travis hopped onto the bed. The orange tom flopped near the duffel and eyed Doyle with mild curiosity. The end of his tail quivered.

"Don't worry," Doyle said. "I'm taking you with me."

The cat yawned. He didn't seem concerned about being left behind.

Doyle went to the bathroom. He grabbed his toiletry bag from underneath the sink and filled it with his toothbrush, shaving gear, and other essentials.

When he returned to the bedroom, his cell phone buzzed on the dresser. Doyle didn't know the number, but he answered it anyway.

"Hello?"

"Hi," a woman said. Her voice was pleasant, with a sing-song lilt. In the background, it sounded as if she typed on a computer keyboard. "Is this Doyle Flanders?"

"It is."

"Hello, Mr. Flanders. This is Louise Klossner with Rally Shipping. You recently placed an order with Big Jake's Seafood Emporium."

"Uh-huh."

For whatever reason, the Marshal Service had created two emergency lines. He contacted one for help and the other contacted him under the guise of follow-up. Doyle wasn't sure why they couldn't use the same number, but he chalked it up to governmental inefficiencies.

"This phone call is being recorded for quality control," Louise said cheerfully. "I hope that's okay."

Doyle grunted.

"I'll take that as your approval," Louise said. "Anyhoo, I regret to inform you there's been a snag with your delivery."

Doyle shoved the toiletry bag into his duffel. "A snag?"

"A delay, but don't worry. Your order is on the way."

"What's the problem?"

"It's not a problem per se." Louise chuckled. The keyboard tapping resumed. "It's embarrassing to tell you this, but our delivery crew was sent to the wrong address."

"How's that possible?"

"It was nothing you did, I assure you. You're a valued customer at Big Jake's. They asked me to pass that along. The mistake was totally on our end. Well, Big Jake's end. They sent us to the wrong address, but it's been dealt with. It won't happen again. You can trust me on that."

"Where was my order sent?" Doyle asked.

"Linda Gata."

"Who's she?"

"She's a city," Louise said with a slight giggle. "It means pretty cat."

So Ekleberry was wrong. *Gato* didn't mean cat. It probably meant gate like Doyle thought all along. He reached out and scratched the cat's head. "Where's this Linda Gata?"

"Just outside Amarillo."

"In Texas?"

"That's the only one I know."

Travis rolled over and swatted at Doyle's hand. The tom's claws caught his index finger and Doyle jerked his hand back. Blood seeped from the cut. "Is there a Fun Time Amusement Park in Linda Gata?"

"No." Louise cleared her throat. "Unfortunately."

Doyle stuck the bloody finger in his mouth. "Then how'd my order get shipped there?"

"The names are very similar. *Lindo Gato. Linda Gata.* You can hear how they could be easily confused."

"Sure, but there's no theme park," Doyle said. "Where did they send my order to in Linda Gata? Does it sound like Lone Star Family Fun Time?"

Louise mumbled something.

"Say that again," Doyle said.

"Sensitivity Training for the Aggressive Male Paradigm. STAMP for short. Their offices are in an industrial park just off the highway, but it's a very popular course with the millennials. I can see by your birthday that you're in that age cohort."

His brow furrowed. "How did my order get sent there?"

"Well, that's a funny story."

"Never mind. I've got it."

Doyle thought of the operator who answered his call earlier, but he couldn't remember the guy's name. It had been a long day, after all. Lots of things came at him. He couldn't be expected to recall the name of one flakey operator. "I hope you fired him."

"As I said, Big Jake's has dealt with the problem."

Doyle didn't like how that sounded. "Does he still have his job?"

"Big Jake's Seafood Emporium is a government-affiliated company, Mr. Flanders. There is a Human Resources process they must adhere to so they can maintain that affiliation status. You understand. Big Jake's can't fire someone willy-nilly. Not even unaffiliated-corporate America can do that anymore and I think we can both agree our country is better off because of it."

Doyle didn't agree, so he kept his mouth shut.

"Anyhoo," Louise said, "that doesn't resolve your issue."

"No, it doesn't."

"So, we here at Rally Shipping have scrambled another team to get your order to you as quickly as possible. They should be there within the hour."

Doyle reached for the cat, but Travis bolted away and jumped off the bed. "It's fine," he said.

"What does that mean?"

"I'm no longer inside the park."

"So..." Louise's voice trailed off as if she was trying to come up with a clever way to phrase her next question.

"I'm safe," Doyle said.

"That's certainly good to hear."

"There's no longer a threat from the Outfit."

"Mr. Flanders," she said sternly, "I must remind you, you're on with Rally Shipping."

"I totally understand."

"So what you're saying," Louise continued, "is you don't need your order any further?"

"No, that's not what I'm saying at all. I would like to have the order diverted."

"Sir, you should have called Big Jake's if you wanted to modify the order."

Doyle's lip curled. "But I just got home. Besides, I didn't have a good experience with Big Jake's."

"I understand, but they've addressed the employee issue."

"I didn't know that."

Louise clucked. "Regardless, there is a procedure to follow."

"To order seafood?"

"Yes. Most definitely. You should have called in and informed a Big Jake's operator that you needed to divert your order."

"Can't I tell you? You're the shipping company."

"That's not how things are done. We have an organizational flow chart. Certainly, you understand."

He didn't. "How about you just have Marshal Krumland call me? He and I will get this mess straightened out in no time."

Louise chuckled. "I'm not sure who you're talking about, and I must remind you we're being recorded for quality control."

"U.S. Marshal Lester Krumland," Doyle said. He loudly enunciated his words. "He's my new witness inspector."

The operator's voice hardened. "Nice work, Mr. Flanders. You just burned another line."

Travis rolled to his back and kicked his feet against Doyle's hand. "So, can I expect a call?"

***

Doyle sat on a kitchen chair he had moved near the front door. He crossed one leg over the other as he read Sara Paretsky's *Indemnity Only*, a paperback he got at a thrift store for seventy-five cents when he first arrived in town. Doyle enjoyed the tale of private investigator V.

I. Warshawski even though the tone was lighter than the Travis McGee and Parker novels he'd recently read.

His duffel was packed, and Travis was in the cat carrier. He could have let the tom roam free, but when his eventual ride showed up, that would have meant chasing the cat down. Better to wrangle him now and be done with it.

Doyle's cell phone buzzed, and he answered it.

"You've sure made some friends today," Max Ekleberry said.

"How's that?" Doyle closed his paperback.

"Lester Krumland called."

"What'd my witness inspector want?"

"For me to violate you."

Doyle tossed the paperback onto the duffel and sat up straighter. Violating his agreement with the FBI meant Doyle would lose his witness protection status and end up back in prison.

"For what reason?" Doyle asked.

"He said you were purposefully tanking your protection placements."

"You know that's not true."

Ekleberry laughed. "Beau, you might have the worst string of bad luck I've ever seen, but you aren't doing this purposefully."

"I appreciate that. Then why are you calling me?"

"Don't lose my number. I have the feeling you're going to need it with this Krumland character."

Beau slid down in his chair and stared at the ceiling. "You think he's out to get me?"

"He's on the hot seat, Beau. His career rests on you holding it together. That's why he wants your agreement torn up and you tossed back into the system. He's pretty upset."

"Today must not have been a gold star for his file."

"Definitely not."

Beau thought about the lost Doyle Flanders identity, the burned call-in line, and the emergency response team sent to Linda Gata because of one operator with hurt feelings. Marshal Lester Krumland was going to have to answer for a lot of actions Beau took today.

"What do you suggest I do?"

"I'd say keep your head down," Ekleberry said, "but I get the feeling you're trying to do that."

"I am," Doyle said. "I really am."

"Then here's what I want you to do. When things go bad next time—"

"There's not going to be a next time."

Ekleberry fell silent for a moment. "You going to listen?"

"Yes."

"When things go bad next time..."

The FBI man waited for Beau to interrupt, but he didn't.

"Because you know something is going to happen," Ekleberry continued. "It always does with you, Beau. And when it does, I want you to call me first. Okay?"

Beau nodded. "Yeah. All right."

"When it does, I'll run interference with Krumland."

"I'd appreciate that."

"Okay, kid. Take care. Let me know where they drop you next."

The FBI agent hung up.

Beau opened the cat carrier and let Travis out. He'd deal with catching the cat when his ride arrived. Right now, he needed to take his mind off his predicament.

He was in the Witness Protection Program with a witness inspector who wanted him kicked out. His only ally was the FBI man who originally arrested him and turned him into a rat in the first place.

Beauregard Smith looked toward the ceiling.

If there was ever a time to swear, it was now

.

Beau Smith
returns in…

Cozy Up
to Mystery

ABOUT THE AUTHOR

Besides writing the Cozy Up Series, Colin Conway is the author of the 509 Crime Stories, a series of novels set in Eastern Washington with revolving lead characters. They are standalone tales and can be read in any order.

Colin is also the co-author of the Charlie-316 series. The first book in the series, *Charlie-316*, is a political/crime thriller and has been described as "riveting and compulsively readable," "the real deal," and "the ultimate ride-along."

He served in the U.S. Army and later was an officer of the Spokane Police Department. He has owned a laundromat, invested in a bar, and run a karate school. Besides writing crime fiction, he is a commercial real estate broker.

Colin lives with his beautiful girlfriend, three wonderful children, and a codependent Vizsla that rules their world.

Learn more at colinconway.com.